The Secret
Laundry Monster Files

The Secret
Laundry Monster Files

John R. Erickson

Illustrations by Gerald L. Holmes

Viking

VIKING
Published by the Penguin Group
Penguin Putnam Books for Young Readers,
345 Hudson Street, New York, New York 10014, U.S.A.
Penguin Books Ltd, 80 Strand, London WC2R 0RL, England
Penguin Books Australia Ltd, Ringwood, Victoria, Australia
Penguin Books Canada Ltd, 10 Alcorn Avenue, Toronto, Ontario, Canada M4V 3B2
Penguin Books (N.Z.) Ltd, 182-190 Wairau Road, Auckland 10, New Zealand

Penguin Books Ltd, Registered Offices: Harmondsworth, Middlesex, England

Published simultaneously by Viking and Puffin Books, divisions
of Penguin Putnam Books for Young Readers, 2002

1 3 5 7 9 10 8 6 4 2

LIBRARY OF CONGRESS CATALOGING-IN-PUBLICATION DATA
Erickson, John R., date.
Hank the cowdog : the secret laundry monster files / by John R. Erickson ;
illustrations by Gerald L. Holmes.
p. cm.
Summary: Hank the Cowdog and Deputy Drover investigate a monster
that appears just as they are about to arrest Eddy the Rac for ripping
one of Sally May's sheets while it hangs on the clothesline.
ISBN 0-670-03541-6 – ISBN 0-14-230076-4 (pbk.)
[1. Dogs—Fiction. 2. Raccoons—Fiction. 3. Ranch life—West (U.S.)—Fiction.
4. West (U.S.)—Fiction. 5. Humorous stories.] I. Holmes, Gerald L., ill. II. Title.
PZ7.E72556 Se 2002 [Fic]—dc21 2001048289

Viking ISBN 0-670-03541-6

Hank the Cowdog® is a registered trademark of John R. Erickson.

Printed in the United States of America
Set in New Century Schoolbook

*Dedicated in loving memory to
Ellen Erickson Sparks, my friend and
sister, who died May 15, 2001.
She liked old Hank.*

CONTENTS

Flapping Sounds in the Night

It's me again, Hank the Cowdog. Being Head of Ranch Security is a full-time job and this time the call came in the dead of night. But before we get to that, I must pass along a very important piece of information. Please listen carefully.

A dog should never fight a raccoon in the water. You know why? Because raccoons are excellent swimmers and pretty good fighters and terrible cheaters, and if they ever catch a dog in the water, they will try to drown him. No kidding. I mention this because it will come up later in the story.

Just keep it in mind as this mystery unfolds.

Now, where were we? Oh yes, the call came in the dead of night. I was in my office, as I recall, yes, in my office under the gas tanks. I was going over a stack of . . .

Okay, I was asleep, might as well admit it, and there's no shame in that. Most ordinary dogs sleep at night, and while I've never thought of myself as ordinary, I do require sleep from time to time. Even your Heads of Ranch Security need sleep.

So I've admitted that I was asleep when Drover turned in the alarm. "Hank? Hank? I hear something out there. You'd better wake up."

I'm not in the habit of responding quickly to Drover's "alarms." He's scared of the dark, don't you see, and if I responded every time he got scared, I would never get any sleep.

Let's be blunt. He's a little fraidy cat. Most of what he sees and hears in the night comes from his own imagination.

So I said, "Leave me alerp. Go awonk. I'm in the midst of a snorking sassafras."

"Yeah, but I hear something out there, honest, and I think you'd better check it out."

"You go cherp it out. I'm bonkers . . . uh, busy. We can tonk about it in the honk. Morning. Go away."

There was a moment of silence. I thought he had given up. He hadn't.

"Hank, there it is again!"

I raised my head and glared at . . . well, I couldn't actually see him, it was so dark, but I glared into the darkness. "Drover, is this another one of your falsely phone alarms . . . phony false alarms?"

"No, this one's real. Listen."

I cranked up Ear Number One and opened the outer doors for Sound Gathering. At first, I heard nothing, but then . . .

"Okay, Drover, I'm picking it up now. It's a scratching sound."

"I'll be derned. What I heard was more of a . . . a flapping sound."

"I hear scratching, not flapping."

"I'll be derned. Can you hear it now?"

I listened. "No. It quit."

"Oh, okay. That was just me. I was scratching."

"Stop scratching! Be still. Silence."

I moved Ear Number One back and forth. Sure enough, there it was—an odd flapping sound in the night. I cranked up Ear Number Two, opened outer doors, and set both ears to Maximum Gathering Mode. The sound came in loud and clear.

"Drover, I don't want to alarm you, but I'm picking up a sound out there in the darkness."

"Yeah, I know. I heard it first."

"It doesn't matter that you heard it first."

"Well, that's why I woke you up."

"You didn't wake me up. I was going over some reports." I pushed myself up on all fours and peered out into the darkness. "Where are we? What day is this?"

"Well . . . I think it's night, and that's why it's so dark. And we're right here under the gas tanks."

"Yes, of course. It's all coming back to me now. Were we just talking about something?"

"Yeah. Those odd sounds out there in the dark."

"Ah, yes." I cocked my ears and listened. There it was again. "Is that the sound you heard?"

"Yep, that's it. Are you proud of me?"

"Oh yes, of course, very proud. And since you're the one who turned in the alarm, maybe you'd like to check it out."

"Yeah, or maybe not."

"What?"

"I said . . . maybe we could go together. I'd like that better. You know, teamwork and stuff."

"Drover, I haven't slept in days. This job is wearing me down."

"Yeah, but I just woke you up, so you must have been asleep."

"I grabbed a tiny nap, Drover. I fell asleep over this huge pile of reports. This Ranch Security work never ends. Be a nice dog and go check this one out. I'll be right here."

"Well . . . okay, I can try." When I heard him take two steps, I collapsed into my gunnysack bed. But he didn't go far. "Hank, there it is again, that sound, and I'm getting scared."

I lifted my exhausted body up from its former resting place. "Okay, spare me the muttering mumble. We'll grumble together on this one, but I'm warping you, Drover. If my health bonks because of this, it will be on your consequence. Conscience, I should say."

"I can handle that."

"What? Speak up."

"I said . . . I just hope I can live with the guilt."

I yawned and stretched. "Okay, this will be a Silent Run. Stay behind me and rig for Night Vision. Let's move out."

And so it was that we, the Elite Troops of the Security Division, left our warm beds and the comforts of home, and moved out into the screaming blizzard.

Wait. This was May. Forget the blizzard. No blizzard. It was a warm night but pretty dark, and into the darkness we crept—the Elite Troops of the . . . I've already said that.

Did we describe the sound? Maybe not. Okay,

here's the scoop. Most of the sounds we pick up in the night fall into three categories: Your Howls (usually coyotes), Your Clanks and Bangs (usually raccoons in the trash cans), and Your Unclassifieds (usually monsters).

This was sounding more and more like a Category Three: monsters. I'm no chicken liver when it comes to patrolling headquarters, but those Cat Threes cause me some . . . well, concern. Monsters are something to be concerned about, right? You bet they are, and right away I was feeling the little pinpricks of fear that often come with Category Three Monster Sightings.

I didn't dare mention any of this to Drover. It would have ruined him for the mission.

We plunged on into the inky black darkness. My eyes and ears were on Full Alert by this time. We followed the sound in a northward direction, bearing two-three-three-zirro-zirro, up the caliche hill and toward the yard gate. By this time, I was getting more complete readings from our sensing devices. The sounds began falling into Subcategory One of Category Three: *flapping.*

Flapping? That was odd. Sometimes we pick up a Sub One Cat Three during the daylight hours, and it always comes from one source: clothes flapping on Sally May's clothesline. But this was the dead of night. I knew for a fact that Sally May never left her clothes on the line at night. Do you know why?

I don't. She just doesn't do it, that's all I can tell you, and I knew for sure that this mysterious flapping sound was not coming from her clothes. It had to be something else.

We continued our stealthy march through the inky blackness, until I suddenly realized that we had . . . BONK . . . arrived at the yard fence. I, uh, picked it up on Smelloradar, don't you see, when I . . . Okay, maybe I ran into the fence with my nose, but the point is that the fence was there and I found it, just in the nickering of time.

I turned to my assistant. "Shhhh!"

"I didn't say anything. I think you ran into the fence."

"I know I ran into the fence, and I don't need you to tell me. What do you suppose is causing that flapping noise?"

"Well, let me think. Could it be clothes on the clothesline?"

"Don't be absurd. Sally May never . . ." I cocked my ear and listened. "It certainly sounds like clothes flapping, doesn't it?"

"It does to me."

"Hmmm. Very strange, Drover. It appears that

we have no choice but to go in and check it out."

"In Sally May's yard?"

"Of course in Sally May's yard. That's where the clothesline is, so that's where we must go."

"Yeah, but dogs aren't allowed in the yard. We might get in trouble."

"That's all changed, Drover. I'm putting the entire ranch under Marshal's Law."

"Who's Marshal?"

"How should I know? Marshal Dillon. Marshal Art. Marshal Mellow. Take your pick. Do you want to sit here and discuss marshals, or get to the bottom of this mystery?"

"Number one."

"Too bad. Saddle up, son, we're going in. I'll go in the first wave. You come in the second wave and guard the rear."

"I wish my rear was back in bed."

"What?"

"I said . . . oh boy, oh goodie, guard the rear."

"That's the spirit. Now remember, we'll have to jump the fence. Can you do it?"

"Well . . ."

"Good, and make as little noise as possible. See you on the other side. Good luck."

Right away Drover started whining. "This leg's killing me."

I ignored his complaints and began the Fence-Jumping Procedure: face fence, coil back legs, spring upward, hook front paws on fence, scramble up and over. I did it without a hitch, then paused and waited for Drover to . . . CLUNK . . . land on top of my head, the little goofus.

I stuck my nose in his face. "Never land on your commander's head, Drover. It's very bad for morale."

"Well, you were in my way."

"It's my ranch, Drover, and I'll stand anywhere I please. We've got six thousand acres here. You're free to land anywhere on the ranch except on top of my head. Is that clear?"

"Well, it was dark. I couldn't see."

"That's not an excuse and this will have to go into my report." I cut my eyes from side to side. "Drover, what did we come here for?"

"Well, let me think. I can't remember."

"This is ridiculous. We went to a lot of trouble to get over the fence. Surely one of us can remember why."

"Not me. I was happy in bed. Wait, hold it, I remember now. I heard flapping but you heard scratching, but it was only me and then you heard flapping too, and we decided maybe it was Sally May's clothes on the clothesline."

"Not likely, Drover. As you may know, she never . . . Did we hold this conversation earlier in the evening?"

"I think maybe we did."

"Ah. That accounts for my feeling of *déjà voodoo.*"

"What's that?"

"It means that we have already discussed this, only we were both half-asleep."

"You mean . . ."

"Exactly. There are no flapping clothes, Drover, and we have entered the yard on a fool's errand."

At that very moment, we both heard a sound that was clear and distinking. Without a doubt, it was the flapping of clothes on a clothesline. The mystery had just taken a turn in a new and sinister direction.

CHAPTER TWO

Unauthorized Rats in the Laundry

ooooooooooooooooooooooooooooooooooooooooooooooooooooo

By this time my head was clear of Post-Sleepal Vapors and my ears were alert to every tiny sound in the night.

Flap, flap, flap.

Those were not tiny sounds. They were loud, sharp reports that perfectly matched our profiles of flapping clothes. I turned to Drover. I could barely make out his profile in the starlit darkness.

Hold it. That wasn't Drover's profile. It was a fence post, which meant that I *couldn't* make out his profile in the starlit darkness. At last we were making some progress.

"Drover, are you there?"

"No, I'm over here."

I whirled around. "Okay, are you there?"

"No, I'm here."

"Here, there, it's all the same, as long as you're where you are."

"Well . . . I am where I am . . . I guess."

"Great. Nice work. Okay, listen up. It appears that Sally May left her laundry on the clothesline overnight. At this point, we don't know why, but I'm beginning to smell a rat."

"They must have been pretty dirty."

"What?"

"The clothes. She had rats in her clothes."

"She did? Why wasn't I informed? Drover, I can't run this ranch without a constant, reliable stream of information. Do you realize what this tiny clue has done?"

"Not really."

"It explains why she left her clothes on the line all night. She found rats in her laundry basket. Don't you get it? She's airing out her laundry. That explains everything."

"Yeah, but there's a cat."

"Wrong, Drover. They were *rats*—unless you're changing your report. You said they were rats. Make up your mind. Were they cats or rats?"

"I'm all confused, but I see a cat."

I squinted into the darkness. It was very dark.

I decided to try a trick question. "What color is the cat?"

"Let's see. Dark."

"Ah! I've exposed an inconsistency in your argument. For you see, Drover, it's impossible to see a dark cat on a dark night."

"Yeah, but I see one. And listen. Now I can hear him . . . yowling."

I probed the dark yard with my Earatory Scanners, until . . . "Holy smokes, Drover, it's a police siren! Someone must have called the cops and they're coming to back us up. Boy, we've blown this thing wide open."

"I think it's the cat . . . yowling."

"Quit talking nonsense. I know a police siren when I . . . Wait a minute, hold everything. Unless I'm badly mistaken, the sound we're hearing is actually the *yowling of a cat!*"

"That's what I said."

"You see, at certain stages and levels, a cat yowl is indesquishable from a police siren. That's a cat you're hearing, Drover."

"Yeah, I know. I wonder who it could be."

"Exactly. And now all we have to do is determine who it might be—and find out why he or she is lurking in the yard. Step aside, son, I'll handle this." I pushed Drover out of the way and marched straight . . . "Uh . . . where was this cat? I seem to be having a little trouble . . ."

"Over there. To your left. Follow the yowl."

"Don't tell me what to do. Of course I'll follow the yowl."

I followed the yowl, using a technique we call Yowl Folleration. You home in on the sound, don't you see, and follow it to the source. At the end of every yowl is a yowling cat. To dogs with very sensitive ears, it's as easy as following a piece of string.

I followed it, and sure enough, at the end of the string of sound, I discovered . . . a cat.

Pretty impressive, huh? You bet. I not only discovered an unauthorized cat lurking in the yard, but within seconds I had given the little sneak a positive identification. You'll be shocked.

It was Pete the Barncat.

I marched up to him. "Okay, Pete, your little game's over."

"Well, well, it's Hankie the Wonderdog. What took you so long?"

"We do thorough investigations, Kitty, and they take time. You can leave now. We know all about the rats in the laundry."

"Oh, really?"

"Yes. Go back to bed and stop yowling. We've got this case under control."

"But there aren't any rats, Hankie."

I stared into his weird yellow eyes. "Hey, Pete, I don't know what kind of con game you're trying to pull, but we were called out for Rat Control. And you know, Pete, if we had a decent cat on this outfit, we dogs wouldn't have to mess with the small stuff. You ought to be ashamed."

"Oh, really?" I could hear him purring, and all at once he began rubbing on my front legs.

"Don't rub on me, you little pest. I hate that and you know it."

"Well, Hankie, I have some information for you. It might help in your investigation. Do you want to hear it?"

"Information from a cat? Ha. No thanks, Pete. We never . . . What kind of information? I mean, I won't use it, I'll ignore it, but just for laughs, what are we talking about?"

"Well, Hankie"—he rubbed and purred and dusted my nose with his tail—"there aren't any rats. You were misinformed."

"Lies, Pete, lies. The Rat Report was turned in by Drover himself. Drover, step forward and tell Pete about the rats."

Drover joined our circle. "Oh hi, Pete. Let's see. Rats. They have long tails and . . . they sleep in laundry baskets and . . . they eat cheese."

I whirled back to the cat. "There! You see? Unless you have some powerful new information, Kitty, we're going to proceed on the basis of Drover's Rat Report."

"Well, Hankie, I do. You want to hear it?"

I stuck my nose in his face. "No, I don't want to hear it. Do you know why? Because cats are not only dumb, but they're sneaky as well. They tell lies, Pete, and you're even worse than most."

"Fine with me. But I'm warning you. That's not a rat over there."

My mind was racing. Was it possible that Pete knew something we didn't know? Not likely, but I had to find out.

"Okay, Pete, I'll bite. I'll take the cheese. Start talking."

He pointed toward the clothesline. "There's a raccoon over there. He's playing with the laundry on the clothesline."

Drover and I exchanged grins. We couldn't keep from laughing.

"Hey, Drover, did you hear that?"

"Hee hee. Yeah, that's the dumbest thing I ever heard."

"Me too. We saw the rats with our own eyes, right? And this cat says it was a raccoon! Next time he tells the story, it'll be a kangaroo."

"Yeah, hee hee." Our laughter faded into silence. Then Drover said, "You know, Hank, I don't think we ever saw the rats."

"What? I thought you . . . ?" I didn't want to discuss Security Division business in front of the cat, so I pulled Drover off to the side for a private consultation. "Look, pal, you're the one who turned in the Rat Report."

"No, I think it was you. I never saw any rats."

"Then what . . . ?" The pieces of the puzzle were beginning to fall into . . . shambles. I gave the runt a withering glare. "Drover, once again your blundering has brought the Security Division to the brink of humiliation. If I hadn't caught this when I did, the cat might have thought we were just a couple of dumb dogs out on a midnight lark."

"Boy, that would have been wrong."

"Exactly, but the weed of truth often grows from tiny seeds." My mind was racing. "Okay, here's the plan. We'll deny all knowledge of the Phony Rat Report. We never heard of it and we know nothing about the rats."

"Except they eat cheese."

"Okay, we know that much, but nothing more. In the meantime, I'll subject the cat to a heartless interrogation. If he knows anything, I'll break him down and wring it out of him. You got it?"

"I guess so. But I think I'm still confused."

"Just keep your trap shut and let me do the talking. Come on."

We marched back to the cat and seated ourselves in front of him. He looked up at us and . . . he was *grinning*. That was pretty positive proof that he was holding something back. Well, I intended to drag it out of him.

"Okay, Pete, we've had a meeting of the board and we've decided to hear your side of the story."

"Oh, thank you, Hankie. I'm so honored."

"You should be. We've decided to make this a special case, so . . . out with it. Keep to the facts and make it brief. We're very busy."

"My goodness, yes, I know you are." He blinked those weird cattish eyes. "There's a raccoon in the yard. He's playing with Sally May's laundry and I think he even ripped a sheet. I thought you dogs might want to know."

"Are you finished? Is that all?"

"That's all, Hankie."

I stood up. "Good. It's another pack of lies and we don't believe a word of it. You're excused. You're free to go chase your tail. Good-bye and good riddance."

Kitty-Kitty gave us one last smirk and a wave of his paw, and then he went slinking back into the darkness where he belonged. When he had gone, Drover and I exchanged grins.

Drover giggled. "Boy, that was even dumber than what he said before. You sure nailed him."

"We must be firm with the cats, Drover, even when it brings us enormous pleasure."

"Yeah, it was fun."

"It was fun, Drover, but the impointant poink

is that we exposed him as a fraud, a cheat, and a liar. In the future we'll know . . . What are you staring at?"

His eyes had moved away from me and seemed to be staring at . . . something. Something in the spoofy darkness of the yard. Spooky, I should say. The spooky yardness of the yard. The spooky . . . Skip it.

He took cover behind me. "Hank, I just saw something move, and I think it was a . . . *raccoon.*"

CHAPTER THREE

We Discover the Ghost from Kalamazooooo

Maybe you think Drover's words went through me like a jolt of electricity, that I was shocked and perhaps even frightened. Not at all. I took it calmly. In fact, I even chuckled.

"Relax, Drover, there is no raccoon in the yard. Shall I tell you why?

"Well, I guess, but he's there, I can see him."

"He's not there and you can't see him. Here's why. Point One. Your credibility as a witness has already been stained beyond repair by your Phony Rat Report. As you know, it caused us great embarrassment and came within a whiskey of making us appear foolish in front of the cat. Whisker."

"Yeah but . . ."

"I'm not finished. Point Two. If there were actually a raccoon in the yard, it would disprove our Theory on Cats. Do you remember our Theory on Cats?"

"Well, let me think here."

"Cats lie, Drover. They always lie. They lie when there's no reason for it. They lie when it would be easier to tell the truth. Hencely, any statement made by a cat is false, period."

"Yeah but . . ."

"If Pete says there is a raccoon in the yard, it means there is *no raccoon* in the yard. The proof is scientific, mathematical, and irreguffable."

"Yeah, but I saw something over there." He cocked his ear and pointed to a rustling sound. "Hear that?"

"I hear it, Drover, and now I will prove that it isn't a coon. Follow me and study your lessons."

We crept forward on silent paws. My eyes were locked on the spot from whence the sound was coming. Closer and closer we crept. I could see him now, the dark outline of some manner of animal or beast, but certainly not a raccoon. He was sitting on his haunches, batting a sheet with his front paws.

In certain respects, his profile resembled a . . .

well, a raccoon, but we already knew that was impossible. Perhaps he was a skunk . . . yes, a skunk who had disguised himself as a raccoon. They do that sometimes, although . . . hmmm . . . it was a very clever disguise. It would have fooled a lot of dogs, but it so happened that I was familiar with their many tricks and disguises.

"Drover, do you smell a skunk?"

He sniffed the air. "Nope, sure don't."

"Neither do I. Do you see what this means?"

"Sure. He's not a skunk, 'cause he's a raccoon."

"Never fall for the obvious, son. These guys are clever beyond our wildest dreams. He's obviously gone to great lengths to disguise his skunk odor. In this business, we have an old saying: the cooner they look, the skunker they are."

"I don't get it."

"It means the more he appears to be a raccoon, the stronger the proof that he's actually a skunk, disguising himself to resemble a coon. Does he look exactly like a raccoon?"

"Yep, sure does."

"There you are. This little creep is a master of disguises, but we must be very careful. Once we expose him and blow his cover, he's liable to give us a spraying. Better let me handle this."

"Fine with me. I still say he's a raccoon."

"What?"

"I said . . . he's playing with a spoon."

"No, that's a sheet. He's batting the sheet."

Drover came to a halt. "Hank, do you see who that is? It's Eddy the Rac!"

I stopped in my tracks and squinted into the darkness. What I saw sent shock waves all the way out to the end of my tail. My mind swirled and tumbled. I felt faint. My legs began to wobble. I had to sit down.

"Drover, rush me to the sewer, I'm a sick dog."

"What's wrong?"

I stared into the emptiness of his eyes. "That's Eddy the Rac. Don't you see what this means?"

"Well . . . I guess not."

I slumped to the ground. My voice had fallen to a croaky whisper. "It means, Drover, that the cat *told us the truth*."

"Yeah, he's a nice kitty."

"He's wrecked my Theory on Cats. I can't go on, Drover, I'm finished. I can't bear to live in a world where cats tell the truth. Good-bye, old friend." I closed my eyes and felt myself slipping out into the dark sea of . . . "Wait a minute." I opened my eyes and sat up. "He did this on purpose, the little sneak. Don't you get it? He knew it would turn my whole world upside down and cause me to doubt everything that is dear and precious." I leaped to my feet. "But it won't work, Drover. We must be strong, even as the rafters of life are crashing down upon our heads. Why are you staring at me?"

"Well, I just . . . I'm kind of confused."

I turned away from his loony stare, gathered my thoughts, then placed a paw on his shoulder. "Drover, being a dunce has its advantages. You're spared some of life's darkest moments. I'm happy for you."

"Thanks. Eddy's tearing up that sheet."

"What?"

"Eddy the Rac. He's ripping up Sally May's sheet."

I blinked my eyes, and slowly my thoughts returned from the edge of the abyss. There sat Drover, the little simpleton, who understood nothing of the terrible crisis I had just endured. "Oh yes. Eddy. Life goes on, doesn't it? Very well, let's place him under arrest."

Leaving the terrible crisis behind me, I took a deep breath of air and returned to my job of protecting the ranch from villains, monsters, and destructive little raccoons. I marched over to Eddy and beamed him a look of purest steel.

"Well, well, it's our old friend Eddy the Rac."

He stopped playing with the sheet and looked

up at me. "Oh. Hi. Found this laundry. What a blast!"

"Eddy, you've come back to the ranch for a little visit, I suppose, and in some ways that's nice. It's touching that you have fond memories of your time here, but one of the things you may have forgotten is that we have laws. One of those laws is *no raccoons in the yard*. Therefore, I have no choice . . ."

"Okay, sure. Hey, watch this." He climbed under the sheet. "I'm a ghost. Woooooo!"

He flapped his arms and made a spooky sound. You know what? Drover fell for it.

"Hank, where'd he go? And look, oh my gosh, there's a ghost!"

He started to run, but I caught him and pulled him back. "Relax, Drover. It's just Eddy. He's playing."

"Yeah, but . . . he was there just a second ago and now . . ."

"I'm telling you, it's Eddy. You know how raccoons are, always goofing off. Here, watch this." I turned to Eddy. "Okay, pal, that's enough. Come out from under the sheet."

"Wooooo! I am the ghost of Kalamazooooooooo!"

The clothespins came unsnapped and the sheet settled over the top of him. He stood up and . . .

hmmm . . . began . . . well, slouching toward us, I guess you might say. I felt the hair rising on the back of my neck.

"Eddy, this has gone far enough. I command you to come out and stop this nonsense at once. Do you hear? Eddy?"

He kept coming. Drover began edging toward the fence. "Hank, I don't like this. Something's happened. Eddy's disappeared and that thing's coming to get us!"

"Drover, don't be ridiculous. Stand your ground and . . ."

I, uh, found myself edging toward the fence alongside Drover. I mean, I was 100 percent sure this was Eddy and not some . . . well, ghost or something, but still . . . okay, maybe I wasn't 100 percent sure, but I was pretty sure this was Eddy, although . . . come to think of it, he didn't look much like Eddy. The thing under the sheet was big and scary and . . . hey, this is a very strange world we live in and a guy hates to take chances with his own life, right?

We crept backward, moving away from the . . . whatever it was, Eddy or a . . . well, a Laundry Monster. Have we discussed Laundry Monsters? They're very rare, and in my whole career I'd seen only a couple of 'em. Our intelligence reports indicated that they're usually peaceful and maybe even playful.

That's at first. Our reports also warned that they should never be approached, because they can turn nasty in the blink of an eye. You've read about grizzly bears? Same deal. Your grizzly bears seem cute and fluffy at first, but suddenly they show their huge teeth and attack. And you know what else? *They eat dogs.*

We had no reason to think this was a grizzly bear. In fact, we were 100 percent sure it wasn't a grizzly bear, but we were beginning to wonder if it might turn out to be . . . well, one of those rare Laundry . . .

He raised his ghostly arms and let out some kind of blurdcuddling moan. Bloodcurdling moan, I should say, and you may not believe this, but all at once I had a powerful feeling that my blood was beginning to . . . curdle. Honest. No kidding.

Well, fellers, this was a very bad sign. I mean, all of our training had taught us to beware of this kind of thing. Let's see if I can remember the exact quote. "At the first sign of curdled blood, a dog should go straight into Code Three Barking. If the curdling process continues for more than two minutes, the dog should seek shelter at once."

There you are, straight out of the Cowdog

Manual of Codes and Procedures. It was beginning to appear that Drover and I had stumbled into a situation that was not only dangerous but also life threatening.

"Drover, I need to ask you a question. At this moment, do you get the feeling that your blood is being . . . well, curdled or something like that?"

"Yeah, I think it is. How about yours?"

"Affirmative. This is worse than I thought."

"I knew it! Oh my leg!"

"I don't want to alarm you, Drover, but it's beginning to appear that we've stumbled right into the middle of a Laundry Monster."

"Oh my gosh. What happened to Eddy?"

"We don't know the answer to that. Maybe the monster ate him."

"The poor little guy!"

"Right. Eddy was a sneak, but I couldn't help liking him."

"And now he's gone."

"Exactly. Now he's gone, devoured bone and toenail by that horrible monster."

"Oh my gosh! Even his toenails? What are we going to do?"

That was the throbbing question that lay before us.

At this time, it's my duty to report that the rest

of this file has to be put under lock and key. It's just too scary for your average reader, especially the kids. Sorry, but the next chapter *cannot, should not, and must not be read by anyone under the age of thirty-five.*

Sorry.

CHAPTER FOUR

The Laundry Monster

Okay, we'll have to check some IDs. Remember, no one under the age of thirty-five is allowed to enter this chapter. I know, it's a nuisance, but we have our rules. Anyone under the age of thirty-five who is caught peeking into this chapter will receive a terrible and severe punishment.

You'll have to stand with your nose in a circle for thirty minutes.

Yes, that's pretty stern, but we just can't allow the Secret Laundry Monster Files to leak out to the general public. Too scary. We can't risk it.

Have we cleared the room of all kids under the age of thirty-five? Okay, I guess it's safe to move on to the scary part.

There we were, Drover and I, surrounded by . . .

well, confronted by this rare and very dangerous Laundry Monster, the likes of which I had never seen in my entire career. I mean, the thing was *huge*. Eight feet tall, maybe even nine. Enormous.

Have we discussed his face? Maybe not, and for good reason. *He didn't have a face.* Honest. No eyes, no ears, no eyebrows, nothing but a long nose that stuck out in front like a . . . I don't know what. Like a cucumber, I guess, or maybe it was a *canister of deadly poison.*

Yes, that's it. They have them, you know. All of your Laundry Monsters come equipped with a canister of deadly poison, and when they bite and sink those horrible fangs into tender flesh, the deadly poison is released into the body of the unfortunate victim.

Any blood that hasn't already been curdled will curdle at once, I mean, immediately on contact. Zippo. Cottage cheese. And you know what happens next? *Your tail falls off.*

Yes, we had ample reason for avoiding a direct confrontation with this fearsome creature. No dog would have risked it, not even Drover who has only a tiny stub of a tail. We continued backing away from him . . . it . . . her . . . whatever it was, until we had backed ourselves into the yard fence. There, we came to a halt. Unfortunately, the creature kept slouching toward us.

By this time I had gone into Fully Raised Hair, which means I had lifted a strip of hair that began at the base of my head and ran all the way out to the end of my tail. Sometimes we have trouble getting those tail hairs to lift, but this time . . . no problem. They were up and ready.

Well, when we felt our hindmost parts making contact with the fence, I knew at once that we had . . . well, run out of yard, I guess you might say, and it was time to make some tough decisions.

"Drover, what's your feeling here?"

"Scared."

"I know, but I mean your feelings about our next move. Should we make a stand and fight to the death?"

"Oh, let's not."

"I'm glad to hear you say that. I mentioned it as one of our options, but I agree that it's not our best. That leaves us with a couple of other responses. I suggest we do a blast of Code Three Barking. If that doesn't stop him, well, we may have to make a run for it. What do you say to that?"

"Let's run first and bark later . . . if we're still alive."

"No. That would bring us some momentary satisfaction, but later we'd look back and regret that we didn't . . ." The monster raised his arms. For a moment my tongue was frozen against the top of my mouth. "Lurr lurr lumlum lurr lurr lum."

"Hank, I can't understand you, help, murder, Mayday!"

"I said, this is getting out of hand. Go straight to Code Three Barking. Ready? Let 'er rip, Drover, give him the full load, don't hold anything back for tomorrow!"

And with that, we braced our legs against the ferocious recoil of the Code Three Barkings and cut loose with a withering barrage. Most monsters can be stopped in their tracks by such a display of bark-fire. Not this one. He kept coming.

"Okay, Drover, that didn't work. He must have raised his Barking Shield. We can't touch him with these barks."

"Who'd want to touch him?"

"Exactly my point. We have no choice now but to abandon our Last Stand Situation and go to a Second-to-Last Last Stand."

"What does that mean?"

"It means *run*, Drover, run for your life! If you can fire off a few barks over your shoulder, so much the better. We've got to sound the alarm. Loper and Sally May must be warned so they can begin evacuating the house. We must save the children!"

"Oh my gosh!"

"We'll regroup on the north side of the house. Ready?"

ZOOM!

Drover was already gone, the little weenie. He'd left without orders, a plan, anything. Our front line had collapsed, our troops were in disarray, it was every dog for himself. I took one last glimpse at the . . . yikes! I cancelled the last glimpse and went straight into the Rocket Dog Procedure—hit full throttle on all engines and went roaring away.

Maybe you think I didn't dare to fire off a few Over-the-Shoulder Barks, but you're wrong. It was dangerous, maybe even foolish of me, but I unloaded several blasts. I knew they wouldn't stop him, but maybe they would slow him down.

Within seconds, I was approaching Light Speed. I streaked around the corner of the house and looked up just in time to see . . . Drover. He was sitting there like a rabbit in headlights, his eyes as big as pies.

"Get out of the way! I can't stop this thing!"

It was too late.

CRASH!

It was a terrible collision. Dogs flew in all directions in a blur of feet, legs, and ears. At first I

feared that the impact had knocked poor Drover all the way out into the horse pasture, I mean, at such speed those collisions can cause unbelievable damage.

I landed in Sally May's flower bed, smashing a whole bunch of . . . uh . . . flowers, so to speak, Sally May's precious flowers. In the deadly silence that followed the wreck, I feared the worst: I was still alive and would be captured by Sally May, who would march me out behind the house and cut off my tail with her butcher knife.

Fortunately, I was spared that awful fate, but then I began to realize that I was badly hurt. I had lost all feeling below my ears. I couldn't move. Perhaps I was paralyzed.

"Drover? Drover, can you hear me?"

His faint voice came from the darkness. "I'm not sure. What did you say?"

"I haven't said anything yet. Are you hurt?"

"Yeah, I got run over by a truck."

"That was no truck, that was me. By the time I saw you, it was too late. Sorry. How badly are you hurt?"

"Terrible. I can't move. I think I'm paralyzed."

"Rubbish. You're not paralyzed. Get up and come here at once."

"Well . . . I guess I could try. Hey, I can move

this foot . . . and this leg moves and . . . oh boy, I can stand up! I'm not paralyzed!"

"See? What did I tell you? Now get yourself over here. We've got a problem."

I heard his footsteps, then his face emerged from the darkness. "Oh, hi. Gosh, you smashed Sally May's flowers. I'll bet she's going to be mad."

"Sally May's flowers are the least of our worries, Drover. We have a much more serious problem than mashed flowers."

"Yeah, that ghost." He ran his gaze through the gloom. "I wonder where he went."

"Shhh, quiet. Our problem is even more serious than the Laundry Monster, Drover. You see, I've been badly injured. I fear that I'm . . . paralyzed."

He stared at me. "That's what I said, and you said 'rubbish.' It kind of hurt my feelings."

"I said 'rubbish' because you *weren't* paralyzed, and I knew it."

"How'd you know it?"

"Because you're a little hypocardiac, Drover. You've spent your whole life being sick and injured, but when it's time to run from a fight, you always seem to do pretty well. My problem is real. I'm in bad shape. If the Laundry Monster comes, I'm afraid you'll have to . . ." I heard a rush of wind. "Drover? Drover! Why you little weasel, come back here at once, and that's a direct order!"

He had abandoned me to my fake. To my *fate*, let us say. My only hope was that the terrible Laundry Monster had given up the chase and had found something . . .

I heard the snap of a twig. My ears shot straight up and swiveled around to the west. I heard the faint rustle of footsteps in the grass.

"Drover? Is that you? If it is, please identify yourself. Drover?"

No answer. The footsteps were coming closer. My heart began to pound and I felt the hair rising on . . . I almost said "on my back," but that was impossible. Don't forget that I was paralyzed, horribly wounded, unable to move. Hencely, the hair on my back couldn't have risen.

It must have been something else.

The sound of the footsteps reached my ears again. I lifted my head and . . . no, wait. I couldn't have lifted my head, right? I must have been mistaken.

In the dreadful silence, I waited and listened. Footsteps, the swish of grass, and then . . .

"I am the ghost of Kalamazooooooooooooo!"

HUH? Holy smokes, he was coming after me!

"Drover, I order you to come here at once, do you hear me? We're moving into a serious combat

41

situation and I demand that you . . ."

He was standing right beside me—not Drover, but the monster, the horrible Laundry Monster. I could almost feel his eerie presence, and then— hang on, this is getting into the heavy-duty scary stuff—I felt the cold, icy swish of his sheet passing across my . . .

That was it, fellers, that's all I could take. Suddenly new reserves of energy poured into my bodily parts and—you might find this hard to believe—my terrible paralysis was . . . well, cured. It was very mysterious, even miraculous, and I don't pretend to understand how it happened, but it did.

Poof! In the brink of an eyeball, somehow the bones in my broken neck welded themselves together and I was back in the Security Business. I didn't waste a second. I leaped to my feet and burned a hole through the darkness and didn't slow down until I had reached a spot just beneath Loper and Sally May's bedroom window.

There, I took up a defensive position and threw the last of my energy reserves into barking a Total Code Three Alert. *Our friends at the house had to be warned.*

"Alert, alert! Alarm, alarm! Ladies and gentle- men, may I have your attention please. We have an enormous Laundry Monster running lose out here. Wake up the children! Get the gun! Evacuate the house at once! This is not a test. Repeat, this is NOT A TEST!"

Having done my duty, I could only wait for help to arrive—and hope that I had warned them in time to avoid a catapestry.

Catastrophe.

(The worst part is over. The kids can come back now.)

The Case Goes Plunging in a New Direction

Lights came on inside the house. I heard the murmur of voices and the pounding of feet. I didn't move until I heard the back door open and saw the glow of the porch light. Only then did I dare to leave my spot and welcome my human friends to the battle.

I crept westward, down the side of the house. As I rounded the northwest corner of the house, I found myself standing face to face with . . . okay, it was Loper. Whew! Boy, was I glad to see him! He was dressed in boxer shorts, cowboy boots, and his felt hat. He carried a flashlight in one hand and a shotgun in the other.

44

The expression on his face was . . . well, angry. Maybe even ferocious. Good. If we had to go up against the monster, we would need all the ferociousness we could mutter. Muster.

He heard me approaching and turned the flashlight . . . ouch! . . . right into my eyeballs. Then he spoke.

"What is it, Hank?"

I did my best to explain the situation. See, I had caught Eddy the Rac playing with a sheet on the clothesline, and just as I was about to place him under arrest, this . . . this HUGE Laundry Monster jumped out of the bushes and . . . and he ATE poor Eddy, just gobbled him down in one bite, and then he . . . he attacked me and I fought him off as long as I could, and then . . . well, I barked for help. That was about it.

Loper threw the beam of the flashlight around the yard. "I don't see anything. Wait." The light fell upon something lying in the grass. It was . . . big and light-colored, with pale stripes.

There, you see? It was the Laundry Monster, I knew it, didn't I tell him? Hey, there was proof, living proof, that I hadn't made this whole thing up.

He walked over and picked it up. It was . . . that is, it appeared to be a . . . sheet. An empty sheet. Loper's eyes came at me like bullets, and he stalked over to where I was sitting. He held up the sheet in front of my, uh, nose.

"What's this?"

Well, it was a . . . sheet, an empty sheet. And it was dirty. Soiled. And torn. But I could explain everything. See, when Laundry Monsters see light or people, they run. And sometimes they run right out of their sheets, so what we had here was the abandoned sheet of a . . . uh . . . former Laundry . . .

Gulp. I had a feeling my story wasn't selling. It was true, every word of it, but who would believe it?

I could feel Loper's gaze burning down at me. I began to melt. My head sank and I gathered my tail between my legs.

"Playing with my wife's clean sheets? In her yard? Well, buddy, I've got some advice for you. Get your little barking self out of this yard, and if you wake me up one more time . . ."

Yes sir, but . . .

He opened the gate. "Out, and don't come back."

Yes sir, but . . . I slithered through the open gate, but not quick enough to avoid his boot on my tail section.

Muttering under his breath, he went back into the house and slammed the door. The lights went out inside the house and silence fell around me.

46

Fine. If that's the way he wanted it, by George, the next time I saw a monster prowling around the house, I would just go back to sleep. What was the point of having a Head of Ranch Security if nobody paid attention to him?

I had never been so outraged. I had risked my life. I might have been killed. The whole family might have been . . .

HUH?

Wait a minute, hold everything.

I put my vast memory banks into Rewind and tried to recall every detail of the night's drama. Eddy was there at the clothesline, right? He was playing with a *sheet*. Only seconds later, we got our first sighting of the . . . of the so-called Laundry Monster, and if my memory served me right, it had been *Drover* who had reported it.

Oh brother! Do you see the meaning of all this? *Eddy was the phony monster!* The little twerp had pulled the sheet over his . . . Drover would pay for this, I mean, I would see to it that he spent the next two weeks with his nose in the corner.

And as for Eddy, the next time I saw him, I was going to . . .

HUH?

I shot a glance to my left. To my right. Who cares? He was standing right there to my left.

Eddy the Rac. Can you believe that? Just as I had figured out his latest scam, he had presented himself for the thrashing he so richly deserved.

He sat up on his haunches, grinned, and waved his paw. "Oh. Hi. How's it going?"

A growl began to rumble deep in my throatalary region. "Why you little cockroach! Did you think you could fool me with that phony ghost business?"

"Wasn't me. Honest."

"Honest? Ha! How dare you use the word? Hey, pal, I had the deal figured out from the start. It was you under that sheet, Eddy, and you thought it would be fun to scare the beejeebers out of us dogs, right? Well, you didn't fool me, not for a minute, and now I'm going to have the pleasure of . . ."

He shrank back and held up his hands in surrender. "Wasn't me. Honest. I can prove it."

I caught myself at the very last second. "You can prove it? Okay, I'll give you one minute to argue your case."

"Five. Give me five minutes."

"No. I'll give you two minutes."

"Four. Just four. Four's all I need."

"Forget it, Charlie. My heart is hard and cold on this deal."

"Three? Three minutes, that's it."

I gave it some thought. "Okay, I'll give you three minutes to prove what can't be proved."

"Great. Thanks."

"And Eddy, even if you prove it, I won't believe it. You know why? Because you're a sneak, and nobody but an idiot would believe anything you said."

"Right. No problem. Here we go." He rolled his little raccoon hands around. "I saw the ghost."

"Ha. I know you did, only you saw him from *the inside*."

"No, outside, just like you. How big was he?"

"How big? Well, I . . ."

"Small? Tiny? Little bitty? Teenie-weenie?"

I gave him a knowing smirk. "Eddy, if you thought he was teenie-weenie, you didn't see what I saw."

"Big, huh?"

"Big doesn't even come close to it. The guy was huge."

"How tall? Three feet? Four feet?"

"Four feet? Ha, what a laugh. No, Eddy, the thing I saw was at least . . ."

"Seven feet?"

"No, eight. He was eight feet tall if he was an inch." I stared at Eddy and suddenly realized . . . "Wait a minute. Is this some kind of trick?"

He must have gotten tired of rolling his hands together, because he reached up and started messing with my ears. That's a raccoon for you. Their hands are always moving.

He gave me a wink. "No trick. How tall am I?"

"I don't know, Eddy, but you're tall enough to reach my ears."

"Eight feet?"

"Uh . . . no."

"Seven feet?"

"No."

"Six feet?"

"Eddy, if you're trying to suggest . . . What's your point?"

He clapped his hands together. "Couldn't have been me. I'm too short. Bingo."

I marched several steps away. He was moving too fast for me. On the one hand, I didn't trust him, not even a little bit, but on the other hand . . .

I marched back over to him. "Okay, I'll admit that what you've said makes a certain amount of sense. The problem is that *you* said it, and I don't believe anything you say."

He threw a finger into the air. "More proof? Fine. That was a king-size sheet, right?"

"I don't know, Eddy, I didn't check the label."

"It was a king-size sheet. Came off a king-size bed, right?"

"Well, I suppose . . ."

"Wouldn't fit me. I wear a pint-size sheet. Wrong size. Bingo." He chirped a squeaky little laugh. "Listen. Got a deal, you and me."

"Hold it, halt, stop! Do you think I'm nuts? Hey, you still haven't convinced me about the monster business, and now you want to talk to me about a deal? What's wrong with you?"

He blinked his beady little eyes. "Sorry. Take your time. I'll wait."

He picked up a weed stem and started chewing on it, while I tried to sort through the evidence he had presented.

Evidence #1: Reliable witnesses had reported the Laundry Monster to be eight feet tall.

Evidence #2: Eddy was nowhere close to eight feet tall. Our careful scientific measurements had established that as fact.

Evidence #3: Other reliable witnesses had reported that the Monster had been wearing a gorilla-size sheet.

Evidence #4: We knew for a fact that Eddy was not a gorilla, or even close to being a gorilla. He was a shrimpy little raccoon.

I paced back and forth, chewing my lip and

thinking deeply on this stunning new twist in the case. Was it possible that Eddy was telling the truth? Only minutes before, I would have scoffed at the very idea. But now . . . hmmm . . . the evidence was impressive, I had to admit that, and even more impressive was that I had gathered it all myself—including the all-important measurement of the Laundry Monster.

That was a solid fact that wouldn't budge. Our best measurement guy from the Security Division had done the work and had taken his readings on a Laser Spyometer. How could you argue against evidence like that?

I stole a glance at the suspect. He had finished chewing up and shredding the weed stem. Now he was juggling three rocks in the air. Eddy couldn't

sit still. Was that a clue? No. It was a fact but not a clue. There's a difference, you know. Some facts are clues and some . . . Never mind.

Having submitted all the evidence to rigorous and heartless analysis, I whirled around and faced the suspect. "Okay, Eddy, we've reviewed all the data and we've reached a verdict. We find you not guilty of the charges of impersonating a Laundry Monster. You're free to go."

For some reason, he started laughing.

The Mysterious
Lost Candy

I stalked over to him and glared into his masked face. "Why are you laughing at the verdict of this court?"

"Just happy. Glad I'm cleared. I was scared, real scared. Know what I mean?"

I allowed the Scowling Muscles in my face to relax. "Okay, Eddy, if that's all it was, we'll accept that. There for a minute, I thought . . . Let me be frank. Every time I'm around you, Eddy, I get the feeling that I'm about to be conned."

"By me? Ha. Couldn't happen. You're too sharp, way ahead of me."

"Well I . . . I wouldn't have put it that way . . . I mean, modesty wouldn't permit me to come right out and say that, but you've raised a good point."

I reached down and gave him a pat on the shoulder. "You've come a long way, little buddy, but you've still got much to learn from the Head of Ranch Security."

"Right. You bet."

"And I'm just thankful that we came through this investigation without any casualties. That Laundry Monster was one of the scariest things I've ever encountered on this ranch. I wonder where he went."

Eddy glanced over both shoulders, then whispered, "Probably still around."

"You think so? He lost his sheet, you know."

"Yeah. Running around naked. He'll be back, steal another sheet."

That opened my eyes. "You really think so?"

"Oh sure. They can't stand to be naked. You know that."

"I do? I mean . . . yes, you're exactly right. It's common knowledge."

"What'll we do? If he comes back?"

I swallowed. "Well, I really don't know. To tell you the truth, I'd hoped he wouldn't."

Eddy started walking to the west. "Better hide. Feed barn."

"Hey, Eddy . . ." He kept going, so I ran after him. "Look, pal, it's easy for you to walk away from a monster attack, but I'm Head of Ranch Security."

He shot me a glance. "Yeah? You saved the house. What'd you get?"

"Well, for one thing, I got the satisfaction of . . ."

"Got in trouble, right?"

"Okay, Loper was a little steamed because I woke him up, but at a deeper level . . . What are you saying, Eddy? Are you saying that . . .? Hmmm, you've got a point there. I mean, I put my life on the line and they yell at me and tell me to shut up my barking."

"Not fair."

"No, it's not fair at all, and sometimes I think . . ."

"Let 'em suffer. Serves 'em right."

"Sometimes I think I ought to walk off the job and let 'em suffer. It would serve 'em right."

"Great idea. Never thought of that."

"Yeah, well, you've never been Head of Ranch Security. You just don't know . . ."

"Right. Injured pride, hurt feelings, stuff like that."

"Exactly. And why should I . . ." I looked around and saw that we were nearing the corrals. "Where did you say we're going?"

"Feed barn."

I stopped. "Wait a minute. Why are we going to the feed barn? I mean, why not somewhere else? Eddy, this isn't one of your famous deals, is it?"

He glanced around and dropped his voice to a whisper. "Can't tell you. It's a secret. You'll see." He walked on.

Well, I had nothing better to do, and I was kind of curious about what his "secret" might be, so I accompanied him down to the feed barn. Do you remember the feed barn? It was an old shed in the southeast corner of the corrals, made of cedar poles and one-by-eight lumber. It had a dirt floor and a tin roof. Since it was handy to the corrals and somewhat weather tight, we used it for storing hay and horse feed.

You might also remember that the door was warped at the bottom, just enough so that a clever dog could wiggle his way inside, in case he . . . well, got in trouble up at the house and needed a place to hide out for a while. I had used it for a hideout on several occasions and it had come in handy.

The only problem with that warped door was that our local raccoons knew about it too, and on several occasions they had broken in and torn up sacks of horse feed, "sweet feed" it's called, because it contains molasses, as well as corn, barley, and other grains. It comes in fifty-pound paper sacks, don't you know, and raccoons love to rip up the sacks.

That was a Major No-No, raccoons getting into the sweet feed, but at the present time it happened to be no problem. Why? Because we were out of horse feed, or almost out. I knew that, because keeping up with all the ranch inventory was part of my job.

And, heh heh, just the day before, I'd heard Loper say that we needed some more feed.

I was curious to see if Eddy knew about the warped door. If he did, it would provide me with information for the future, just in case the feed barn was ever raided again. If it was, I would already have one suspect on my List of Suspects.

I mean, in some ways Eddy was a nice little guy, but in my line of work, we have no friends. Everyone is a suspect and we're always on the alert for new pieces of information.

That's just part of being a top-of-the-line, blue-ribbon cowdog. We never lose that instink for protecting the ranch. We care, even when there's no reason for caring.

Anyways, I hung back and watched to see if Eddy knew the secret combination for entering the feed barn. Aha! Just as I had begun to suspect, he went straight to the door and . . . well, stopped. He sat down and began rolling his busy little hands.

"Gosh. Door's shut. Can't get in."

Chuckling to myself, I nudged him out of the way and took the lead position. "Eddy, I'll show you a little trick, if you'll promise never to reveal it to any of your thieving friends and kinfolks. Watch this." I dropped down on my belly and slithered my way through the crack. "Now, let's see if you can do it."

He squeezed through the crack, but not nearly as gracefully as I'd done it. That told me something pretty important. Eddy had never raided the feed barn before. That was good news.

Well, once inside the feed barn, I felt free to sit down and relax. "Whew! Boy, what a night. Eddy, I sure thought we'd lost you to the Laundry Monster." I heard him make an odd sound. "Are you laughing?"

"Oh, no. Allergies. Cough, cough! See? Ragweed."

"The ragweed doesn't make pollen until late summer, Eddy."

"Wheat dust."

"They won't be cutting wheat for another month."

"Sporophonic particles. You know about those?"

"Sporophonic . . . oh sure, those things. Yes, they cause coughing and sneezing, don't they?"

"Bad. Terrible. Cough, cough! Cough, cough!"

"Hey, you'd better take care of that cough, pal. It sounds pretty . . ." He reached up and started poking one of his fingers into my ear. "Would you mind not doing that? How can I show concern for your health when you're sticking fingers into my ear?"

"Sorry. Got bored. You know me. Moonlight Madness. Moon's up, I got to move. Daylight comes, I'm zonked."

I moved away from him. "Yes, we've been through this before, Eddy—goof off all night, sleep all day, and blame it on Moonlight Madness. It's part of being a raccoon, and it's something you must learn to control."

His little eyes were shining. "Listen. Got a deal. Garbage barrels. Quick job, in and out, no heavy lifting."

"No. We did a garbage job the last time you were here. Do you remember who got caught and sent into exile? Me."

"Okay. Garden. Raid the garden. Corn, lettuce, okra, great stuff."

"No. The corn isn't ripe and I don't eat okra or

lettuce. No deals, Eddy. Just try to relax and be a nice law-abiding little raccoon."

He heaved a sigh. "I get bored. Hey. You smell something?"

I sniffed the air. "No, I don't . . . Yes, I do smell something. It smells pretty good, doesn't it? I wonder what it could be."

I heard him sniffing the air again. "Candy."

"Ha, ha. I don't think so, Eddy. See, this is a *feed* barn, not a candy barn. If this were a candy barn, it might be full of candy, but since . . . sniff, sniff . . . since that smell is so sweet, we must consider the possibility that it might be, uh, candy. What do you think?"

"Right. Sweet. Candy."

"One of the cowboys might very well have left some candy in here."

"Sure. Hiding it. That's it."

"Exactly. He was trying to hide it and . . . No, wait, I've got an even better explanation. Listen to this." My eyes prowled the darkness, just in case we were being watched and monikered. Monitored. Eavesdrope. Listened to. "One of the cowboys was down here working, see, and he had a bag of candy in his pocket. He bent over to pick something up and the candy slid out of his pocket."

"That's it! And now we smell it, right?"

"You've got it, pal, that's it, the whole story."

"Should we eat it?"

"Hey, Eddy, you know what they say about Finders Keepers? 'Finders keepers use their beepers.'"

"Beep, beep!"

"Huh? Was that you, Eddy? I just heard, well, a beeping sound."

"Right. Beeper went off."

"Well, that settles it, doesn't it? If your beeper went off, that makes us Finders Keepers, right? That's further proof that the Mysterious Lost Candy was meant for us."

"Wow. What a mind. Wouldn't have thought of that. Should we eat it?"

"You bet your life . . . that is, if we can find it in the dark."

"No problem. I'll find it. Watch." I heard him sniffing and patting his hands in the dark. Then . . . "Got it. Candy, big bag of candy."

"Great. Is it still in the wrapper?"

"Yep. Paper wrapper."

"That checks out, doesn't it? Do you suppose we can tear it off and get to the candy?"

He squeaked a little laugh. "Hee, hee. No problem. I've got hands."

RIP!

"Hey, Eddy, that was a big rip."

"Right. Big bag of candy. Real big." I could hear him gobbling something. "Oh yes! Want a bite? Great stuff."

"You bet I do. Hey, we found it fair and square, Finders Keepers, right? Don't hog it all, Eddy, here I come!"

CHAPTER SEVEN

Okay,
Eddy Tricked Me

Wasn't it amazing that we'd found a bag of candy in the feed barn? Who'd have thought it? Not me, but we sure did, and boy, was that some bodacious-good candy!

Delicious. In the dark barn, Eddy and I set ourselves to the task of devouring the Finders Keepers Candy that we'd found and kept. It was ours, fair and square, and though it was too bad Slim or Loper had lost it, their loss was our, heh heh, snack.

We smacked our way through that candy. It was a little dry, but great stuff. It wasn't chocolate, as you might have supposed. I mean, a lot of your average candy is covered with chocolate, but this was no average candy. It had the taste of . . . well, molasses. Molasses and plenty of nourishing whole grains, which was a pretty strong hint that this was some of your Health Food Whole Grain Finders Keepers Candy.

That's the best kind, you know. Your average candy is just made of sugar and junk, but your Health Food kind contains a long list of ingredi-ums that build strong bones, red blood, long whiskers, and sleek hair.

And you know what else? It was a BIG bag of candy. Eddy had said it was big, and he'd been right on the mark. Biggest bag of candy I'd ever experienced. Huge. We ate and ate and ate, and still there was more.

At last I had to stop and rest. "Whew! Man alive, Eddy, are we done yet?"

"Nope. Got more. Good, huh?"

"Oh yeah, great stuff. But how do you suppose that thing ever fit into a shirt pocket?"

"Big shirt. Big pocket. Want some more?"

"No thanks, I'm stuffed. Help yourself, pal, I've just about . . ."

HUH?

The first light of dawn's first light was show-ing through the cracks in the barn, and some of the light was making its way inside, which meant that I was now able to see my business partner and also the bag of candy that we had . . .

I stared at the bag of so-called candy. "Hey, Eddy, I thought you said that was Health Food candy."

"Nope, not me. Didn't say that."

"Okay, but you said it was candy. I heard you. That's what you said. Well, look what we've been eating. Do you see what I see?"

He sat up on his haunches and began licking his paws. "Candy?"

"Why you little . . . that isn't candy. We've been eating the last sack of *horse feed*!"

"Pretty good, though, huh? Hee hee."

"No, it wasn't good. It was terrible. I hated every bite, and do you know why? Because, Eddy, stealing horse feed on this ranch is a *serious crime*."

"Gosh."

"And any dog who got caught stealing horse feed would be in big trouble."

"Gee whiz."

"And if we get caught in this barn with a plundered sack of sweet feed, you'll think gee whiz." I leaped to my . . . that is, I tried to leap to my feet, but something had happened to my . . . my belly had grown, shall we say, and all at once . . .

Fellers, I was so stuffed with stupid horse feed,

I could hardly walk! I jacked myself up to a standing position and waddled over to him.

"Okay, Shorty, this does it. You and I have come to a parting of the waves. I should have known."

"What's the problem?"

I stared into his beady little eyes. "What's the problem? You tricked me, Eddy. Once again, you tricked me and forced me to eat half a sack of forbidden horse feed."

"Sure was easy."

"It was easy because you convinced me it was candy. How dumb do you think I am?" There was a long throbbing silence. "Okay, I was dumb enough, but never again, Eddy. Once dumb, twice smart. We're through, finished. If the cowboys find this mess, I'll have no choice but to confess that you did it. I'm leaving now, and with any luck at all, we'll never see each other again. Good-bye."

Without looking back or feeling even the slightest hint of regret, I marched straight to the crack in the door and . . . hmmm . . . found that I was too fat to squeeze through the crack. I marched right back to Eddy.

I cleared my throat. "Eddy, you remember what I said about never wanting to see you again?"

"Yeah, sure."

"I was misquoted. My words were taken out of

contacts. What I really meant to say was . . . hey, pal, I'm so stuffed, I can't squeeze through that crack in the door. Do you suppose you could lend a hand? I mean, we've been through a lot together."

"Yeah. The Laundry Monster."

"Right, the terrible Laundry Monster. We stood together on that one."

"Scary guy."

"Exactly. He was a very scary guy, but we hung together and fought him off as a team, Eddy. We make a great team and . . . well, I guess you know what would happen if the cowboys found me here."

He nodded. "Sure. ZZZZITTT!" He ran his finger along his throat.

"Exactly. It would, uh, look very bad, so I was wondering if you might . . ."

"Sure. No problem." He monkey-walked over to the door and pried open the crack.

I followed, walking like . . . I don't know what. Like a big fat tomato. "You're a great guy, Eddy, I've always said so." I tried to squeeze through the crack. "Wider, Eddy, open it just a little wider. More. Pull harder." I heaved and grunted and finally popped out on the other side. "Thanks, bud. You never could have done this without me."

"No problem."

Then I stuck my nose in his face and raised my lips in a snarl. "And now, you little creep, get off my ranch and don't ever come back."

"Gosh. What about the team?"

"Our team is finished. Furthermore, it never existed. I was tricked into this shabby affair, and my report will deny that I had any involvement whatsoever. And if you ever show your little outlaw face around this feed barn again, I'll have to place you under . . ." He reached out a paw and twisted the end of my nose. "What are you doing?"

"Too loud. Turning down the volume."

"That's not a volume knob. That's my nose."

"But it worked. Hee hee."

"Okay, so it worked, but that's because I have nothing more to say to you. Our team is dissolved, Eddy, our partnership is finished. Go away and leave me alone. Good-bye."

I turned away from the little sneak and marched . . . well, waddled away. I mean, I was so full of horse feed . . . I walked away, is the point, and turned my back on the guy who had brought me so much grief and had done his very best to ruin my life.

Well, I had just pulled the ranch through another dangerous night, filled with strange sounds, howling coyotes, prowling raccoons, and

Laundry Monsters. It had been a toughie, and maybe you think I went back to bed. No sir. At exactly 0641 I barked the sun over the horizon and turned that department over to J. T. Cluck, the Head Rooster.

As a rule, chickens are dumb and incompetent, which is the mainest reason why I never trust J.T. or any other chicken to bark up the sun. We also have the fact that chickens can't bark, and even if they tried, it would be a silly bark, certainly not enough to force the sun over the horizon.

No, barking up the sun is a job for the Head of Ranch Security, and chickens need not apply. On the other hand, once I've taken care of the heavy lifting—heaving the sun over the eastern horizon—I don't mind turning it over to J.T.

He has a small talent for crowing, don't you know, and he does okay, once I've got the sun on the road. He stands there in front of the machine shed, puffs himself up, and spends fifteen or twenty minutes making silly motions with his neck and squawking at the sun.

It's all pretty dumb, seems to me, but it doesn't cause any great harm, and I guess it gives his hollow little chicken life some meaning.

Anyways, I left a few small chores for J.T. and hoofed it down to my office-bedroom beneath the gas tanks. I was bushed, exhausted, worn to a frazzle by a night of dangerous work. I went straight to my gunnysack, scratched it up a few times, and collapsed.

You might have noticed that I didn't take the time to do the procedure we call Circle the Bed. That gives you some idea of just how exhausted I was. Circle the Bed is extremely important, and there are many reasons why we do it. Hmmm. But at the moment, I can't . . .

There are many important reasons why we circle our beds, but I'm afraid they are so secret and classified, I can't reveal them. No kidding. You never know who might be listening. In this line of work, we must be very careful. As we say in the Security Business, *the ears have eyes.*

The walls have eyes.

The walls have EARS.

There we go. *The walls have ears,* and we never know to who or whom those ears might belong, but they always seem to come in pairs—the ears do—and when they happen to belong to someone in our vast network of enemies . . . well, it can be very dangerous.

I'm not allowed to say any more about this. If our enemies ever discovered the reasons why we circle our beds . . . I'm not even allowed to speculate. It could lead to a huge breach in our Security Apparatus, and the consequences could be . . .

Sorry, that's all I can say.

You'll just have to go on wondering why we circle our beds, and if anyone asks if we discussed this, please deny any knowledge of it.

Okay, where were we? I don't remember.

Something.

Chickens? No.

The weather? I don't think so.

This really annoys me.

Wait, here we go.

I had just returned to my office after a long night of . . . so forth, and collapsed on my gunnysack bed. I was spent, exhausted. I had given my best energy to the ranch and now there was nothing left. I needed sleep. My whole body cried out for sleep.

As I curled up into a ball of fur and turned out the lights of my mind, I became vaguely aware that Drover was there beside me, sleeping his life away on his gunnysack. He was making certain odd noises, such as "honk," "wupp," and "snork," in his sleep. I made a mental wupp of these pork chops and began snorking the . . . muff mirk sassafras . . . zzzzzzzzz . . .

It Was a Pickup, Not a Liberian Freighter

Perhaps I dozed off. Yes, I'm almost sure I did, and for the very best of reasons. I was bushed, but we've already discussed that, so let's move along.

I must have slept for several hours. In my line of work (I'm Head of Ranch Security, have I mentioned that?), in my line of work, it's rare that we get a chance to sleep two or three hours without an interruption. This time it happened, but then it came to an end, as it always does.

I heard a vehicle approaching the ranch.

Traffic Control is an important part of my job around here, so staying in bed was out of the question. My left ear shot up, even as the rest of my body clung to sleep, and soon a stream of data was flashing back from Data Control's massive computer center.

Our initial report suggested that the unidentified vehicle was . . . a Liberian freighter? Hmmm. That seemed odd. I mean, a freighter is a kind of boat, a ship, and ships are usually found on oceans, right? My ranch is located in the Texas Panhandle, and if you'll move over here into the Map Room . . .

Well, maybe you can't do that, but if we were in the Map Room, I would point to a map of the Panhandle and you would notice right away that we have no oceans. We don't even have many lakes. We do have a creek, but it's not very deep, certainly not deep enough for . . .

Okay, it appeared that we were getting garbage reports from our instruments, so it was necessary for me to move into Alert Stage Two. This required that I lift my head and, most difficult of all, crank open the outer doors of my eyes, which allowed me to . . . well, look out and see things.

I blinked my eyes several times, did a Visual Sweep of . . . Okay, we were facing the wrong direction, so I went to the huge effort of swiveling my head around to the east, and it was then that I saw . . .

It wasn't a Liberian freighter. It wasn't any kind of freighter. It wasn't even a boat, which confirmed my first response to this alert. What I saw was . . . what I saw was . . .

Saw was? Have you ever noticed that if you spell "saw" backward it becomes "was"? I found this very interesting. Could it be some kind of clue or coded message?

I decided to wake up Mister Sleep-Till-Noon and get a second opinion.

"Drover, wake up. I have a very important question to ask you." He didn't wake up. He mumbled and honked and muttered in his sleep, so I went to sterner measures and barked in his ear.

Heh heh. I must admit that I get some wicked pleasure in waking up Drover. You never know what the little mutt will say or do. This time, his head shot up and his eyes popped open.

"Oh my gosh, help, murder, Mayday! I think she loves me but flypaper comes in rolls." He stared at me for a moment. "Oh, hi. I thought you were Beulah, and you just said you were crazy in love with me."

"No. I'm not Beulah and I don't love you. And if anyone's crazy around here, it's you."

"I'll be derned. There for a minute . . . You're not Beulah?"

"No. I've already said that. You're babbling in your sleep."

"Yeah, but I'm not asleep."

"Okay, you're awake and babbling, which is even worse."

"Gosh, maybe I was asleep."

"I just said that."

"You did? When?"

"Just now."

"Huh. I must have been asleep. I didn't hear a thing."

I heaved a sigh. "Drover, please be serious and try to concentrate. This could be very important. I want you to listen to two words and tell me if you think they could be part of a secret code."

"Okay. Am I supposed to pick the words?"

"No. I'll pick the words and you will listen. At that point, you will give me your opinion."

"Now?"

My lip curled into a snarl. "Wait until I give you the words, tuna."

"Oh. Okay. Sorry."

"The two words are . . ." I glanced over both shoulders, just to be sure our conversation was secure and confidential. We never know who might be dropping the eaves. "The two words are . . . *saw was*. Do you see anything unusual about those words?"

"I can't see 'em at all."

"Okay, do you *notice* anything unusual?"

"Well, let me think." He wadded up his face and rolled one eye around. I guess that meant he was concentrating. "If a guy had one sawa and then got another sawa, he'd have two sawas. I guess."

I stared into the emptiness of his eyes. "There is no such thing as a sawa, Drover, and if one sawa doesn't exist, then we can't possibly have two sawas."

"I think I'm confused."

I rose to my feet and began pacing in front of him. "Yes, Drover, either you're confused or else you take some fiendish pleasure in slowing down my investigations. I'm trying to involve you in my work. I gave you a chance to state your opinion, and what did you do?"

"I don't know. I was asleep."

"Of course you were asleep. You're always asleep. That's one of your biggest problems. But every once in a while, Drover, we must wake up and smell the taffy."

"Boy, I love taffy."

I whirled around and drilled him with my gaze. "Hush, not one more word. Now listen carefully. Do you realize that *saw* is *was* spelled backward? The two words are mirror images." He stared at me. "Hello? Is anybody home in there?"

"I thought it was taffy."

"What?"

"You said I had to smell the taffy."

"Forget the taffy, Drover. The two words are mirror images of each other."

"Yeah, but I don't have a mirror."

I heaved a huge sigh and walked a few paces away. Was I going insane or was he? I couldn't tell, but at least one of us . . . I had tried to ask the runt a simple question and somehow he had managed . . .

At that point, I made an important decision. I left Drover on his gunnysack and hurried away, got as far away from him as I could get, before he infected my mind with . . . whatever it was.

Chaos. Typhoid fever.

Make no mistake about it. That's a weird little mutt.

Oh, and I decided that the whole business about *saw was* meant absolutely nothing. It was gibberish, a rabbit trail without a rabbit.

On the other hand, we most certainly did have an unidentified vehicle approaching ranch headquarters. That turned out to be a very important piece of information, and it soon led me into unwatered charts.

Uncharted waters, I should say. The unidentified vehicle soon led me into uncharted waters.

You see what Drover does to me?

Okay, now we're cooking. Once I had a strong visual sighting of the vehicle, I knew that it was no Liberian freighter. The clues were everywhere. First, there was no ocean, no beach, no water, no jellyfish. Second, the vehicle had wheels and was moving down the road, which made it virtually impossible that it could be a ship. And third, I suddenly realized that the whole business about the so-called Liberian freighter had been a product of my . . . uh . . . sleeping mind, as you might say, and was therefore absurd.

I even had to face the possibility that my loony conversation with Drover had been partly my fault.

But the important thing was that I had just intercepted an unidentified vehicle as it was creeping toward our ranch compound, and I wasted no time in sounding the alarm. Near the front yard gate, I issued Warning Barks. When the vehicle didn't slow down or flee in terror, I advanced to the next stage in the Readiness Procedure. I hit Full Flames on all engines and went . . .

My goodness, it appeared that a cat had just walked into my path. How sad! How unfortunate! Do you see what this meant? It meant that unless I went to some trouble to alter my course, I would probably . . . heh heh . . . give the kitty a "plowing," shall we say.

Run over him. Bulldoze him.

Now, wouldn't that be too bad? I would have felt terrible about doing such a thing, but you must remember that once we go into the Full Flames procedure, it's very hard to make even the tiniest corrections in our course.

Okay, maybe it's not all that hard, but only if a guy wants to go to the trouble of doing it. And I didn't. You know why? That wasn't just any ordinary cat up there. It was Pete, the same little creep who had told me the truth only hours before and had ruined my Theory on Cats. And now he would pay.

Heh heh. He didn't see or hear me coming. I wasn't surprised. See, cats aren't very smart. In fact, they're *dumb*. But even more important, they often walk around with their eyes closed and their mind on other things. They purr while they walk, stick their tail straight up in the air, and they have no idea what's going on in the rest of the world.

What was going on in Pete's world was that I was streaking out to intercept a strange vehicle, and he just happened to be walking along in my path. Or close to it. I had to make a few course

83

corrections to get a good clean shot at him, but that was no big deal. Heh heh.

VROOOOM!

Reeeeer! Hiss!

Yes sir, I got him bulldozed, ran right over the top of him and sent him rolling. As I roared past, I yelled back over my shoulder, "Oops, sorry, Kitty, but I'm on my way to a Code Three!"

He picked himself up off the ground and glared ice picks at me through the cloud of dust. I loved it! What a wonderful way to start the day.

Yes sir, I was feeling terrific, but now that I had plowed the cat, I had to turn to more important matters—the unidentified vehicle that was approaching headquarters. I turned all sensory devices toward the front and began gathering clues and targeting information.

Green and white Chevy pickup, bearing two-four-zirro-zirro.

Pretty impressive, huh? You bet it was, but there's more. At that point, I also went into Stage One Barking. We have several stages of barking, don't you see, and Stage One is the . . . well, the first stage, and maybe that was obvious, but what wasn't so obvious was that we also have a Stage Two, a Stage Three, and a Stage Four.

Stage One is the first of many stages, in other words, and we use it to alert the trespasser that he has been picked up on the Security Division's vast radar network. A lot of times your trespassers will give up at this point—stop the vehicle and jump out with their hands in the air.

And sometimes they don't. When they don't, we know we've intercepted a hardhead, and we move straight into the higher stages of barking.

When this happens, things get very tense, and on a few occasions, we've had to go to the drastic measure of shooting out their tires with tooth lasers. No kidding.

But this guy seemed to realize that he was in Big Trouble. As I swooped in and confronted him with a withering barrage of Stage One Barking, he coasted down the hill and . . .

"Get out of the way, fool!"

. . . pulled up to the yard gate. Yes sir, he knew he'd met his match and he was smart enough to surrender before we had to do some destruction to his pickup.

At that point, you probably think that he stepped out of the pickup. No, that's not what he did. Hang on and you'll see.

CHAPTER NINE

The Lovely
Miss Trudy Arrives

The stranger didn't step out of his pickup right away. First, he *opened the door.* Only then did he step out. See, if he hadn't opened the door . . . Never mind, but sometimes these tiny details are pretty important, I mean, if he hadn't . . .

He opened the door and stepped out, is the point, and then and there I was able to amass a complete description: tall, skinny, a clean pressed western shirt, blue jeans, dark eyes, new straw hat, and . . . hmmm, very interesting. He was wearing a pair of *yellow boots,* and they were not only yellow, but they also had little bumps all over 'em.

This struck me as very strange. I mean, I'd spent my whole career around guys who wore cowboy boots, but I'd never seen a pair that was yellow and bumpy. What was the deal here?

Did I dare dart in for a thorough Smellonalysis? I lifted my gaze and studied the stranger. He was tucking in his shirt. Oh, and he slapped at a spot of dust on his jeans. In other words, he wasn't paying any attention to me, which meant that I might have just enough time to swoop in and give the boots a thorough sniffing.

Maybe you think this was a waste of time, sniffing a guy's boots. Well, under ordinary conditions, I might agree, but there was something odd going on here. What exactly were those little bumps on the surface of the leather? Maybe you hadn't thought of that, but consider the possibilities.

Those bumps might have concealed *tiny microphones* or some other sensing device that we had never seen before. They're very clever, you know, our enemies. Just when we think we've solved all their tricks and disguises, they come up with something new . . . and possibly menacing. We must stay on constant alert and leave no sturn untoned.

At that very moment, Drover arrived on the scene—huffing and puffing and late. "Oh, hi. Did I miss anything?"

"Shhhh! Of course you missed something. You always miss something because you're always late."

"Yeah, this old leg . . ."

"Never mind the excuses. You missed the First Wave, you're late, and thus, you have no idea what we're watching in this case."

"Oh, you mean the yellow boots?"

"Right. Because you dawdled around, you couldn't possibly have known that we're alarmed about those . . ." I gave him a withering scowl. "How did you know about the yellow boots? Who told you?"

"Well, nobody told me."

"Ha! You expect me to believe that? Out with it, son, I want to get to the bottom of this barrel. Was it the cat?"

"Was what the cat?"

"Was it the cat who tipped you off about the yellow boots? I must know, Drover. This could be very important."

"Well, let's see here. No, it wasn't the cat. He got run over by a passing dog."

"That was me."

"Oh. You sure rolled him."

"Thanks. Go on."

"Well, he rolled about ten feet and got up, and that was all."

"What about the yellow boots?"

"No, he was barefoot."

My eyes rolled up into my head. "Drover, please try to concentrate. Who told you about the yellow boots?"

"Well, let me think here. Yellow. Boots. Yellow boots. I don't know."

"Then why did you mention it? There must be more to this than meets the eyeball."

"Okay, I'm working on it." He wadded up his face and wrinkled his nose. "I saw the yellow boots and I thought they looked . . . funny."

"Funny? You mean, funny ha-ha?"

"Ha, ha. Ha, ha."

"Why are you laughing?"

"I don't know. You laughed and I thought . . ."

"I did not laugh, and do you know why? This is no laughing matter. It could be very serious."

His face acquired a very serious expression. "There, is that better?"

"Much better. Now get to the point. Who told you about the yellow boots?"

"Well . . . nobody. I just saw 'em and they looked . . . yellow."

"Ah! Now we're getting somewhere." I began pacing, as I often do when my mind is driving toward a solution. "The boots looked yellow. Tell this court what thoughts or feelings came to your mind when you saw the so-called yellow boots."

"Well, let me see here. I thought . . . I thought they were the yellowest boots I'd ever seen."

"Good. The boots looked yellow, therefore you assumed they *were* yellow, is that correct?"

"I guess so."

"Good. We're getting close to something. One last question, Drover. Did you happen to notice the tiny bumps on the surface of the alleged yellow boots?"

"Oh yeah, I saw 'em right away. Ostrich boots always have bumps."

I stopped my pacing and turned my head slowly around. "Wait a minute. Are you saying that man's an ostrich? Because if that's what you're saying, Drover, I must warn you . . ."

"No, they're ostrich *boots*."

I heaved a sigh and searched for patience. "Allow me to point out a floy in your ointment. Cowboys wear cowboy boots. Ropers wear roper boots. Hikers wear hiking boots. Following this path of simple logic, who or what wears ostrich boots?"

He rolled his eyes around. "I'm confused."

"Ostriches, Drover."

"You mean, he's an ostrich?"

"No! That's my whole point. And if he's not an ostrich, those can't possibly be ostrich boots. You said they were ostrich boots. Therefore, you are wrong, wrong, and wrong."

"I'll be derned. I thought they were."

"They're not, and I will now prove it beyond a shallow of a doubt."

Let me pause here a moment to say a word about my conversation with Drover. You might have found it a bit confusing. Don't worry. So did I. Talking with Drover often leads to feelings of confusion.

See, on a certain level, it might have appeared that we were arguing about whether or not the owner of the yellow boots was an ostrich. No. That would have been a foolish argument, for the simple reason that the owner of the boots was obviously NOT an ostrich. He was a man, a human person.

What Drover neglected to say in his pathetic attempt to argue his case was that the whole discussion came down to the subject of *leather*: were the boots made of ostrich leather or ordinary cowhide leather? Thus, when he made the claim that the boots were "ostrich boots," he was referring to the leather, not to the occupant.

Is it clear now? I apologize for this mix-up, but I must tell you that this is typical of Drover. He has a tiny mind and he is careless in his use of words. The result is often bedlam and confusion.

Now, where were we? Oh yes, he had just made

the claim that the stranger's yellow boots were made of "ostrich leather." This, of course, was outrageous. In the first place, ostriches are birds, right? Yes, they are birds, large birds with long skinny legs and equally long and skinny necks. In the second place, it is common knowledge that boot leather does not come from birds, whether their necks are skinny or not.

Boot leather does not come from birds. Period. Has anyone ever heard of "hummingbird boots" or "mockingbird boots" or "chicken leather boots"? No sir. If it has wings and pin feathers, it's a bird and you can't get leather out of it.

Ostrich skin boots? I had never heard of anything so ridiculous. And to prove it once and for all time, I marched over to the stranger and proceeded to give his boots a thorough Sniffospectral Analysis.

Sniff, sniff.

Aha! Just as I suspected. Our preliminary report showed a strong reading of *boot leather,* and no reading whatsoever for chickens, birds, ostriches, or . . .

BONK!

He kicked me on the nose. The cad flicked the toe of his left boot in such a way that it rammed into our sensitive testing equipment! And then he said—this is a direct quote—he leaned over and said, "You leave a wet nose print on my new ostrich boots, Shep, and I might make another pair out of your hide. Scram. Scat!"

Sure, fine. Hey, if he had something against the march of scientific research, if he wanted the world to be plunged into darkness and ignorance, that was his problem, not mine. I had tried to do my job. I had made a sincere attempt to shine the light of scientific truth into the darkness of . . . something . . . and by George, if he wanted . . .

Wounded and saddened by this shabby affair, I turned away from his stupid yellow boots and marched back to Drover.

And my name wasn't Shep.

CHAPTER TEN

Fresh Evidence
of a Raccoon Attack

Drover was grinning.

"Why are you grinning? That man just set the march of scientific research back twenty years. My investigation ended in failure."

"No, he gave the answer. Don't you remember?"

"I remember nothing but a sudden rush of pain on the end of my nose."

"Well, he said . . . Let me think here . . . He said, 'You leave a wet nose print on my *new ostrich boots* . . .' That's the answer. They're ostrich boots, and I was right. Are you proud of me?"

I held him in the gaze of my watering eyes for a long moment. I hardly knew what to say. "So that's it, huh? You're going to believe him over me?"

"Well . . . they're his boots. He ought to know."

"Yes, but his boots are on *my* ranch. Had you forgotten that? As long as his ridiculous yellow boots are on my ranch, they are *not* made of ostrich leather, period. Do you know why? Because I refuse to believe that you can make boots out of bird skin."

"Well . . . I guess that's all right with me. What are they made of?"

"They're made of . . ." I cut my eyes from side to side. "They're made of porcupine skin. Porcupines are cowardly animals, and therefore yellow. Do you see the connection?" He stared at me with crossed eyes. "I wish you wouldn't cross your eyes at me. It gives me the feeling . . ."

At that very moment, the front door opened and Loper walked out of the house. He stepped off the porch and came down the sidewalk. He met the stranger at the gate and they shook hands. I was observing all of this and taking mental notes of every tiny detail. Here, let's give a listen.

Loper: "Morning, Joe Don. Those are some mighty pretty boots. Ostrich?"

Joe Don: "Yep, full quill ostrich. Bought 'em yesterday on sale."

Okay, stop the tape. You'll notice that this "Joe Don" fellow continued to insist that his yellow boots were "ostrich," an obvious lie and fabrication. At that point we weren't sure why he wanted to conceal the fact that they were made of Cowardly Porcupine, but notice that he revealed a very crucial piece of information. Maybe you missed it.

Full quill.

Do you see what this meant? I'll give you a hint. What kind of animal has *quills*? Heh heh. Not an ostrich, fellers, but a PORCUPINE. Didn't I tell you? Didn't I tell Drover? Yes, with that tiny revelation, I had blown the Case of the Yellow Boots wide open.

Pretty impressive, huh?

Okay, back to the tape.

Joe Don: "Where do you want this horse feed?"

Loper: "Down at the feed barn. Slim's down there somewhere. Holler and he'll help you unload it."

And that was it. Joe Don climbed into the pickup, in the back of which was a big stack of bagged horse . . .

HUH?

Yes, the bed of the pickup was stacked high with fifty-pound bags of feed, but there was something else in the back of that pickup, and there's no way you will ever guess what it was.

I was shocked, amazed, astammered when I saw it.

Or should I say . . . HER.

It was a woman. A lady dog.

She was a blond cocker spaniel, and fellers, when I saw her up there in the back of Joe Don's pickup, I felt myself melting into a big puddle of dog hair. I mean, she wasn't just pretty, she was *gorgeous*!

Description: long blond hair, big brown eyes, a darling little nose, long curly eyelashes, great ears, teeth, and paws. Oh, and she had a red ribbon

perched on her lovely little head. She was a knockout, the prettiest lady dog I'd seen in months or years, and after catching that first glimpse of her, I knew that she was the Woman of My Dreams.

At this point, you may be asking yourself, "But what about Miss Beulah, Missy Coyote, Miss Scamper, and all the other lady dogs in Hank's life?" Well, they too were Women of My Dreams, but this was, well, a different dream.

I caught a brief glimpse of her before Joe Don fired up the motor and drove down to the feed barn. There I stood in the cloud of caliche dust, too startled to move, too smitten by love to utter a sound.

Drover was there beside me, and I had every reason to suppose that he, too, had just been hit on the head by the Cinder Block of Love. He's a copycat, you know, especially when it comes to the ladies. He's always trying to butt into my romances. Where he gets the idea that a lady dog might be interested in him, I don't know.

Well, yes, I do know. He's immature and has a wild imagination.

I heaved a sigh and stared off at the pickup. "Drover, did you see what I just saw?"

"You mean, the horse feed?"

"Not the horse feed. The lady dog."

"Oh, her. Yeah, I saw her. Boy, what an ugly dog."

Slowly, I turned my head around and held him in my gaze. "Ugly? What are you talking about?"

"Well . . . she's a Pekingese, and I think they're kind of . . . ugly. You know, their noses are pushed in."

"Drover, any dope can see that she's a cocker spaniel."

"No, I'm pretty sure she's a Pekingese."

"Tell you what, Drover. Let's march down to the feed barn and settle this thing once and for all. I will ask her myself."

And so it was that we left the area in front of the house and marched ourselves down to the feed barn. I was still feeling a bit . . . uh . . . full, shall we say, and perhaps I wasn't marching as crisply as usual. Drover noticed.

"Gosh, you're sure walking funny. And you look kind of . . . fat."

"Don't try to change the subject, Drover. The problem with you is that when you see a beautiful lady dog, you lose your head. It's a sign of immaturity, you know."

"I'll be derned."

"You need to work on those things."

"Okay. But you still look . . ."

"Hush."

At last we reached the feed barn. Joe Don had

backed up the pickup in front of the door and Slim had joined him. Both men began carrying . . .

Oops. I suddenly remembered the, uh, phony candy. Maybe you'd forgotten about that, and maybe I had too, but . . .

I heard Slim's voice. "Dadgum raccoons! They got in here and tore up a whole sack of feed."

Hmmm. Obviously he'd found the evidence of . . . of Eddy's penetration of our feed barn. I rushed inside and studied the cream of the crime.

The *scene* of the crime, shall we say, and yes, Slim was right. The raccoons had torn up a whole sack of horse feed. I was shocked and outraged. I began whipping my tail from side to side, and beamed Slim my Look of Deepest Concern.

"Hank, where were you when the coons busted in here and tore up this sack of feed?"

Well, I . . . Far away. Out on patrol. Nowhere close to the, uh, feed barn. No kidding.

"Well, pooch, we'll be storing twenty sacks of feed in here, and I'd advise you . . ." His voice trailed off, and it appeared that he was staring at . . . well, at ME. "Good honk, what have you been eating, an inner tube?"

Who, me? No, I certainly had not eaten an inner tube. No.

His eyes narrowed. He glanced down at the

sack of—yipes—at the plundered sack of feed. Then his eyes swung back to me. "Surely you didn't . . . Nah, dogs don't eat horse feed."

There! Did you hear that? It had come straight from Slim's mouth: *Dogs don't eat horse feed.* In other words, I had been cleared of all the suspicions and false charges against me, and I was free once again to beam Looks of Outrage at the damage created by the outlaw raccoons.

What a mess! Why, there must have been two or three of them . . . maybe even five . . . a whole gang of barn-wrecking raccoons, and through Angry Wags and facial media, I beamed the message to Slim that *this would never happen again.* Not on my watch, not while I was in charge of Ranch Security.

Boy, I was really mad. Imagine those thuggish raccoons, stealing feed right under my nose! They would pay for this.

The men went back to the job of unloading the feed, and though I was so outraged about the plundered feed that I could hardly speak or think of anything else, I . . . uh . . . tore myself away from the scene of the crime and turned my attention to . . .

WOW!

I could see the lovely lady dog sitting up on the tool box, watching the men. Even at a distance, the earthquake of her beauty sent a tremor through my heart.

I marched up to the pickup and let my adoring gaze float up to her. "Well, my goodness, look what we have here. A lady dog has come to visit our ranch. Afternoon, ma'am, I'm Hank the Cowdog, Head of Ranch Security."

She saw me and . . . she SMILED! "Oh, hi. I'm Trudy. I stay in town."

"Ah, Trudy, what a special name! Hey, listen to this." And with that, I sang her my special Trudy song. Have we ever done it before? Maybe not. Here's how it went.

Trudy, Trudy, What a Beauty!

Now Trudy, you have caused a stir among
    us dogs today.
We're all excited, all shook up, we don't
    know what to say.
Drover thinks you're Pekingese, he says
    your nose is pugged,
But I don't care, O gorgeous one, my heart
    has just been mugged.

Trudy, Trudy, what a beauty.
Makes me think of more than duty.

I sure hope that you're not snooty, Trudy.
Perhaps you'll be my sweet patooty.

Cocker spaniel, that's my guess, I love
    your floppy ears,
One look at them and right away my mind
    was stripping gears.
Your stringy hair is fixed just right, I love
    those liver lips.
A kiss from them could cause a wreck and
    sink a thousand ships.

Trudy, Trudy, what a beauty.
Makes me think of more than duty.
I sure hope that you're not snooty, Trudy.
Perhaps you'll be my sweet patooty.

I see that you are smirking and it's
    causing me some pain.
Perhaps you think I've lost my mind and
    really gone insane.
Well, maybe so but you're the cause, for
    showing up out here.
Those big old cocker spaniel eyes have
    knocked me on my rear.

Trudy, Trudy, what a beauty.
Makes me think of more than duty.

I sure hope that you're not snooty, Trudy.
Perhaps you'll be my sweet patooty.

That got a smile out of her. I knew it would. "Well, lawsy me! Did you make it up yourself? It rhymed and everything, didn't it?"

"Oh sure. Rhymes come easily to me, Miss Trudy, for you see, they come straight from my heart."

"Ah, no fooling? That's sweet. But you're too fat for me."

I moved closer. "Fat? Hey, I can explain . . . Ma'am, I must tell you that I'm not the kind of dog who falls in love at first sight, but . . ." I noticed that her gaze was wandering, so I shifted my plan of attack. "Miss Trudy, I wonder if I might ask you a question."

She glanced away. "I guess so. Sure."

"You see, Miss Trudy, my assistant and I were having a little debate. Now, we both agreed that you're gorgeous"—I gave her a secret smile—"but we couldn't agree on whether you're a cocker spaniel or a Pekingese. I wonder if you could . . ."

She perked up. "Who's your assistant?"

"His name's Drover, but that's not important. The point is . . ."

Her eyes widened. "Is that . . . *him*?" She pointed

her paw at . . . well, in the general direction of . . .
okay, she seemed to be pointing toward Drover,
who was sitting off by himself and gazing up at the
clouds. Her mouth bloomed into a smile, which I
thought was very weird, and then she said, "Oh,
my! Oh, my, my, my! He's so . . . keeee-yoooot!"

CHAPTER ELEVEN

The Toad Factor

Drover heard this. His stare moved down from the clouds and rested on Miss Trudy. He gave her a goofy smile and waved his paw. "Oh, hi."

She rushed to the edge of the tool box and looked down. "So you're Drover?"

"Yes ma'am, that's me, just plain old Drover."

"Oh, my." She giggled. "You're about the cutest little thang I ever saw."

Drover's eyes popped open. "Me? I'll be derned. Hank, did you hear that?"

I gave him a withering glare. "I think it's time for you to patrol the chicken house."

Trudy heard this. "You do patrol work?"

Drover grinned and started wig-wagging his

stub tail. "Oh yeah, all the time." He gave me a grin and came over to the pickup.

I cleared my throat. "About that song of mine, Miss Trudy . . ."

They ignored me, both of them, just as though . . . I couldn't believe it. Drover walked right in front of me and started talking to her.

"Yes ma'am, I do patrol work all the time."

She fluffed up her ears. "Oh, how interesting!"

"Yeah, when we have stuff that's really dangerous, Hank lets me do it."

Her eyes glistened. "Honest? How daring! Don't you ever get scared? I mean, what about dark nights?"

Drover puffed himself up. "You know what, Miss Trudy? The darker the night, the better I like it. Sometimes during the day, I get bored and I just wish the night would come—black dark night with no moon."

"Oh, this is so interesting! What about coyotes? Do you ever see coyotes at night?"

"You bet. When they get too close to the house, I go out and . . . beat 'em up."

She gasped and looked at me. "Does he really?"

"Ha! Are you kidding? Miss Trudy, I must warn you . . ."

She turned back to Drover. "Oh, this is just . . .

Well, what about thunderstorms, Drover? They just scare me to death."

"Not me. I bark 'em away. And I bark at the mail truck, too. And you know what, Miss Trudy? Last night I caught a Laundry Monster in the yard— and I whipped him."

On hearing this, the brainless Miss Trudy went into such a swoon, she almost fell out of the pickup. Fortunately, the men had finished unloading the horse feed by then and Joe Don was ready to go back to town. Otherwise, we would have been forced to listen to more of this shameless rubbish.

As Joe Don pulled away, Miss Trudy rushed to the back of the pickup and waved good-bye to her... whatever he was. Her new windbag boyfriend.

"Bye-bye, Drovie. I think I love you!"

Drovie? Oh, brother.

When they were gone, Drover heaved a sigh. "Gosh, that's the cutest lady dog I ever met."

I glared at him. "Drover, she's uglier than mud. Did you see that nose?"

"Yeah, I loved it!"

"She's obviously a Pekingese, and it's common knowledge that Pekingese have a pushed-in pug nose that is anything but cute."

"No, I think she was a cocker spaniel, and they have the prettiest ears in the world."

"A cocker spaniel? Are you nuts? Drover, anyone with eyes could see . . ."

I heard a clunk and turned around. Drover had fainted and that was the end of the conversation. It was just as well. The runt had obviously made a complete fool of himself over an ugly Pekingese dog, and I could feel nothing but pity for him.

Well, the blind, unbalanced, tasteless Miss Trudy had come and gone. Her presence on the ranch had lit a brief spark of meaning in the black hole of Drover's life, but now it was time for us to get back to work.

As the dust cloud left by the pickup settled, Slim came out of the feed barn and latched the door. "Hank, come here."

Upon hearing my name, I snapped to attention, left the fantasy world of Drover's childish folly-rot, and trotted over to Slim's side. I had a feeling that I had been summoned, not for social reasons, but for a matter of great importance. I was right.

"Hank, there's a hundred bucks' worth of horse feed in that barn. I've got a suspicion that them coons'll be back tonight."

Oh yes, the thieving, scoundrelous raccoons.

"It wouldn't be funny if they got in there and tore up all them sacks, would it? I want you dogs to guard the feed. You hear?"

Yes sir! I was the right dog for that job. I had no use for raccoons and would be proud to protect our ranch's supply of horse feed from the thieving rascals. As soon as darkness fell, I would be right there at the barn door, waiting for a foolish raccoon to show himself.

Slim went back to work, and guess who came rushing up at that very moment. Mister Love-Struck. Mister Keeee-Yooooot. Drover.

I shot him a hot glare. "Well, I see you made a miraculous recovery. I guess that tells us all we need to know about your so-called romance."

"Yeah, it was pretty exciting."

"It was superficial, Drover, and your behavior smacks of insincerity." Suddenly he began smacking his lips. "Why are you doing that?"

"Well . . . I'm not sure."

"I just said that your behavior smacks of insincerity, and you smacked your lips. Are you trying to be funny?"

"I don't think so. I'm so much in love, I don't know what I'm doing."

"Then pay attention to me, because I know exactly what I'm doing."

"Oh good. What are you doing?"

I glanced over both soldiers and lowered my voice to a whisker. "Drover, we have good reason to believe that those thieving coons will be back tonight."

"You mean Eddy?"

"Exactly. Eddy and all his kinfolks. You see, Drover, after you abandoned me to the Laundry Monster last night, I followed Eddy to the feed barn. And . . . I caught him *stealing horse feed.*"

"Oh my gosh!"

"Shocking, isn't it? And he'd eaten so much, he was as fat as a toad." I noticed that Drover's gaze went to my . . . well, to my midsection, you might say. "What are you staring at?"

"Oh, nothing. You look kind of . . . fat, is all. Almost as fat as a . . . toad."

There was a long moment of silence, and the tension in the air between us grew very tensionous. Then I broke it with an easy chuckle. "Ha, ha. Oh, I get it now. I said that Eddy was as fat as a toad, and you noticed that I'm as fat as a toad, and from that you concluded . . . ha, ha . . . you actually thought that I ate the horse feed?"

"Well, I wondered."

"Ha, ha." I gave him a fatherly pat on the shoulder and eased him away from the, uh, feed barn. "Drover, I'm proud of you. That was an excellent piece of observation."

"Gosh, thanks."

"You're learning to put your clues together. That's good, but in this particular case, the clues are just a little deceiving."

"They are?"

"Yes, for you see, there's a missing piece to the puzzle."

"I'll be derned."

"And for the sake of your education, I'll reveal it to you." We stopped. I looked over both shoulders and lowered my voice. "But you must promise never to breathe a word of it to anyone." He nodded. "Drover, this morning at first light, I discovered a toad sitting near the yard fence. I hadn't eaten in days and I was starving, so I . . ."

His eyes grew wide. "You ate a toad, and that's why you look as fat as a toad!"

"Nice work, son, you figured it out."

He was hopping up and down. "I couldn't believe you ate horse feed with the raccoons."

"No, it was just a toad, and that explains everything, doesn't it?"

"Yeah, it all fits together, except . . ." His grin melted. "Why would you want to eat a nasty toad?"

"Drover, that is a great question, no kidding, but I'm afraid we're out of time. We'll save it for another occasion, for you see"—I ran my gaze over the western horizon, where the sun had just

dropped behind a line of cottonwoods—"night is coming, and I guess you know what that means."

"Raccoons?"

"Right. We've got a job to do. Let's move out."

Whew. Having dodged that little bullet, I took a solemn oath to whip the stuffings out of the first raccoon who showed himself. And I hoped it would be Eddy. The little sneak.

When darkness fell, we were in position and ready to mount our defense of the feed barn. I was tense and ready for the battle to begin. If the raccoons were foolish enough to test our position, they would learn some bitter lessons about Ranch Law.

The minutes passed slowly, then stretched into hours. No one came. The hours stretched into more hours and . . . hmmm, I found myself drifting off to . . . well, not exactly drifting off to sleep, but edging toward a, uh, napping situation, shall we say.

I leaped to my feet and began doing exercises. "Drover, let's talk. I'm getting sleepy."

I heard him yawn. "Okay. What shall we talk about?"

"Anything. You pick the topic."

"Oh good. You know, we never did find out if she was a Pekingese or a cocker spaniel."

"Who? Oh, her. She was a Pekingese, Drover, and I wasted a perfectly good song on her too."

"Yeah." He yawned. "She sure was pretty."

"She was ugly, and also not very smart."

"Yeah, she had the prettiest eyes I ever saw."

"Could we change the subject?"

"Well, sure, okay." He yawned. "How come you ate that toad?"

"Toad? For your information, I've never . . . Oh, yes, the toad. I was hungry. What else can I tell you? Hunger drives us to irrational behavior."

"Yeah, and so does love. The first time I saw her, I thought she was just an ugly little mutt, but then . . ." He yawned again.

"Will you please stop yawning? You're liable to get me started . . ." I yawned. "There, see what you've done? Now I'm yawning. If we're not careful, we'll find ourselves . . ." I yawned. Drover yawned. "Keep talking, Drover, but I don't want to hear any more about your ugly girlfriend."

"Okay." He yawned. "Let's see here. I think she loves me, and the snorker I mork, the snicker the pork chop."

"That's the donkiest thing I ever heard, Drivel. In the first plunk, murk wumple the pumpkin waffles."

"Grasshoppers fly banana airplanes."

"Yes, but lorkin murgle snork sniff."

"Sniffle wiffle woebegone mufflers."

"Zzzzzzzzzzzz."

"Zzzzzzzzzz."

CHAPTER TWELVE

You'll Never
Guess the Ending

Okay, let's skip to the bottom line. In spite of our best efforts to stay alert, at some point after midnight, the entire Security Division . . . uh . . . fell asleep. Or to put it another way, we finally succumbed to the crushing burden of protecting the ranch from dangerous forces, and the next thing we knew . . .

I heard a sound in the darkness. My head shot up and my ears went into Automatic Liftup. I shook the vaporous vapors out of my head and listened. There it was again.

A scratching sound. Whispers. Chuckles and giggles. The mysterious sounds were coming from . . . the feed barn.

I turned to my snoring, wheezing assistant.

118

"Drover, wake up. This is it. The raccoons are here and I'm putting the whole ranch under Red Alert."

His head came up and his eyes drifted open. "I thought you said the grasshoppers were flying banana airplanes."

"No, I did not say that. I said the feeds are about to attack the raccoon barn. Now get up. We're fixing to get ourselves into some combat here." He tried to run away, but I caught him. "And this time, mister, you stay on the front line with me. We just might need all our troops for this one."

"Darn."

"What?"

"I said, 'barn.'"

"That's correct. At this very moment, they're attempting to enter the barn. Now listen, here's the plan. I'll take the big one. You take the little ones."

"What if they're all big?"

"If they're all big, I'll take the biggest big one and you take the littler big ones."

"Yeah, but you said . . ."

"Will you dry up? Just jump in there and bite somebody. And don't forget, Drover, this is for the ranch."

"You know what? I don't think you ate a toad.

I think you and Eddy ate the horse feed, and that's how come you're so fat."

I stared at him with eyes of purest steel. "Drover, that's the dumbest thing you've ever said in your whole life."

"Yeah, but it's true, isn't it?"

"The fact that it contains a tiny particle of truth doesn't change the fact that it was a dumb thing to say. But I'm going to forget you ever said it."

"Thanks."

"Now, let's teach these little beggars a lesson they'll never remember. A bold defense of the feed barn will save my reputation, and there might even be a little promotion in it for you."

"Oh goodie. When do I get it?"

"Later. Saddle up, we're moving out."

And with that touching interlude behind us, we went creeping through the creepy darkness to engage the raccoons in deadly combat. Ten yards out, I started getting a red warning light on the Locator Panel. A quick glance at the VizRad scope (Visual Radar) told me that we had three cunning little Charlies (coons) standing near the barn door.

I switched over to our Emergency Radio Frequency. "Okay, Drover, we've got three Charlies dead ahead on course two-five-zirro-zirro. I'll take Fatso. You take the others. Ready? We're going in." I abandoned my Stealthy Crouch and went streaking toward the enemies, with guns blazing. "Freeze, turkeys! You're under arrest!"

Ha. You should have seen their faces. They were shocked beyond belief, scared out of their wits. The dummies had thought they had the place all to themselves, never dreaming that our Raccoon Recon Squad had been observing them for hours. Raccoons have the reputation of being pretty smart, but in a combat situation, they're no match for a couple of high-dollar cowdogs.

You know what they did? They ran. Hey, I'd hoped we might get ourselves into a little scuffle, but these little twerps wanted none of us. They fled in sheer terror. I can't be sure, but I think it was the "freeze, turkeys" that got 'em.

I fell in behind the big one. "Okay, Fatso, here's what we think of feed-stealers and barn-wreckers!"

I jumped right onto the middle of his back, figured the weight of my enormous body would put him on the ground, but . . . well, fat guys don't go down as easily as you might suppose, and he sort of gave me a piggyback ride . . . all the way down to the creek.

I was a little surprised, to tell you the truth, and all at once I found myself in a pool of water with this . . . you know, he'd looked fat and pudgy at a distance, soft and slow and not terribly threatening, but . . . well, after riding him down the creekbank and into the water, I began to see him in a different, uh, flame of reference.

He wasn't fat, fellers, he was BIG. Maybe he had a roll of fat on the outer layer of his body, but mostly what he was was big. Stout. Muscular. Hard as twenty-five rocks. Oh, and he also had a real nasty personality. And a mouthful of teeth.

We were out there in the middle of this pool, see, a fairly deep pool of water. We were paddling around, and he was glaring at me and grinning an evil grin. Drover had come to the edge of the pool and was yipping his little head off.

"Git 'im, Hankie, git 'im! Frozen turkey! Frozen turkey!"

And this giant coon said to me, "Say, bud, you know how a raccoon drowns a dog?"

"Why no, I, uh, don't know . . . about that."

"First, he lures a dumb dog into a pool of water. You know why?"

And once again, I found myself puzzled. "No, this is all new to me. Why?"

"On dry land, a dog can whip a raccoon. Guess who wins in the water."

I ran that one through my data banks. I felt a

jolt of electricity burning its way out to the end of my tail. I heard myself gulp. "Are you saying that, uh, coons are better swimmers?"

"Yeah."

"And that in hand-to-hand combat in a pool of water, the raccoon might have a . . . uh . . . slight advantage?"

"Big advantage."

"And that the raccoon might actually . . ." I hit right full rudder, went to Flank Speed on all engines, and headed for the nearest bank. "Drover, I don't want to alarm you, but I've just decoded this guy's secret message and it's time for you to do something—fast!"

He jumped up and down and yipped louder than ever: "Frozen turkey! Frozen turkey!"

"Never mind the frozen turkey! Don't you see what he's fixing to do? If you don't get yourself out here and do something to help, he's going to *drown me!*"

That ruined him. "Oh my gosh, Hank, don't let him do that!"

"Swim out here and help me, you little squeakbox, and maybe he won't!"

"Yeah but . . . you know about me and water. And this old leg just went out on me."

"Hurry up, do something, attack!"

"Okay, Hank, just hang on a little longer. I'll run for help."

"What? No, don't run for help! Swim out here and . . ."

BLUB. GARGLE. BUBBLE. BLUBBER.

Uh-oh. Fellers, all at once I was in big trouble. The raccoon caught up with me, jumped on top of my head, and put me down where the fish live— and where dogs don't.

Pretty scary, huh? You bet it was, but just then something happened. All of a sudden, the raccoon . . . well, released me. I floated to the surface, grabbed a gasp of air, and realized . . . hmmm . . . that someone or something was towing me across the pool. I mean, some unknown hero was pulling me through the water by one ear.

Did it hurt? Yes. Did I complain? No sir. By George, whoever that guy was, he could pull my ear any time he wanted.

I made it to the east bank, coughed some of the water out of my guzzle, and staggered to my feet. "Listen, pal, I don't know who you are or why you happened to show up, but I sure am . . ."

Imagine my surprise when I squinted through the darkness and saw the face of . . . a coon? Yes, it was a raccoon: sharp nose, black mask, beady little eyes, rounded ears. But it wasn't Fatso. I could see

that at a glance. He wasn't fat, see, and that was a major clue. He appeared to be quite a bit smaller than Fatso and . . . then it hit me like a tub of bricks.

"Eddy? Eddy the Rac? Is that you?"

He dipped his head and waved a paw. "Hi. How's it going?"

I harked up some more water—and moss and seaweed and two lobsters. "How's it going? Well, up until about thirty seconds ago, it was going fast— down the drain of life. I was about to get myself drowned by one of your kinfolks."

"Yeah. That was Bubba. Second cousin. Likes to fight."

"I noticed. He also likes to cheat."

"Hates dogs. Never fight Bubba in the water."

I sat down on the bank and beamed him a stern glare. "That's great advice, Eddy. Too bad you weren't around ten minutes ago when it might have done some good."

"A dog can't beat him in a water fight."

"Could we change the subject? The next time I have a chance to fight your lard-tailed cousin in the water, I'll find something else to do, okay?"

"Sure. No problem."

"But never mind. You saved my life, Eddy. I don't know why you did it, but . . ."

"Dead dogs mess up the water hole."

". . . but I'm honored that our friendship meant so much to you. I mean, it almost brings tears to my eyes to know that you didn't want me stinking up your water hole."

"Right. And I've got a deal."

I stared into his masked face. "What? You've got a . . ." I started backing away. "Okay, Eddy, thanks for the help, but nix on the deal. Sorry."

"Garbage job. Easy work. In and out, no problems."

"A garbage job? Are you nuts? The last time we pulled a garbage job, well I don't even want to think about that. Good-bye, Eddy. Thanks again for your help and I'll see you down the road." I didn't wait to hear any more. I turned and ran away from the Voice of Temptation who had done his best to ruin my life.

But then I stopped. "Hey Eddy, one last question, and I want the honest truth."

"Sure. Go for it."

"Truthfully, honestly, and earnestly . . . were you the Laundry Monster?"

He chirped a little laugh. "Me?"

"The whole truth, Eddy, no matter how much it hurts. I have to know."

"Sure. Okay." He rolled his little hands together. "Nope. Wasn't me."

"Just as I thought. Thanks, pal, see you around."

And that's about it. Next morning, Slim and Loper found coon tracks around the door of the feed barn and I received the ranch's highest award for bravery. I had run the Laundry Monster off the ranch and had saved the horse feed from the marauding raccoons. Pretty amazing, huh? You bet it was.

Case closed.

Oh, and that business about me and Eddy eating the horse feed? Ha, ha. Nothing to it. Just a nasty rumor. Don't forget, I ate a toad. No kidding.

Dogs don't eat horse feed.

Have you read all of Hank's adventures?

Join Hank the Cowdog's Security Force

Are you a big Hank the Cowdog fan? Then you'll want to join Hank's Security Force. Here is some of the neat stuff you will receive:

Welcome Package
- A Hank paperback of your choice
- Free Hank bookmarks

Eight issues of *The Hank Times* with
- Stories about Hank and his friends
- Lots of great games and puzzles
- Special previews of future books
- Fun contests

More Security Force Benefits
- Special discounts on Hank books and audiotapes
- An original Hank poster (19" x 25") absolutely free
- Unlimited access to Hank's Security Force website at www.hankthecowdog.com

Total value of the Welcome Package and *The Hank Times* is $23.95. However, your two-year membership is **only $8.95** plus $3.00 for shipping and handling.

☐ Yes, I want to join Hank's Security Force. Enclosed is $11.95 ($8.95 + $3.00 for shipping and handling) for my **two-year membership**. [Make check payable to Maverick Books.]

Which book would you like to receive in your Welcome Package? Choose any book in the series.

(#   )   (#   )

FIRST CHOICE   SECOND CHOICE
_____

                                        BOY or GIRL
_____
YOUR NAME   (CIRCLE ONE)

_____
MAILING ADDRESS

_____
CITY   STATE   ZIP

_____
TELEPHONE   BIRTH DATE

_____
E-MAIL

Are you a ☐ Teacher or ☐ Librarian?

Send check or money order for $11.95 to:

Hank's Security Force
Maverick Books
P.O. Box 549
Perryton, Texas 79070

DO NOT SEND CASH. NO CREDIT CARDS ACCEPTED.
Allow 4–6 weeks for delivery.

The Hank the Cowdog Security Force, the Welcome Package, and The Hank Times *are the sole responsibility of Maverick Books. They are not organized, sponsored, or endorsed by Penguin Putnam Inc., Puffin Books, Viking Children's Books, or their subsidiaries or affiliates.*